Winter Roads, Summer Fields

Winter Roads, Summer Fields

Stories by
Marjorie Dorner

Drawings by
Allan Servoss

MILKWEED EDITIONS

© 1992, 2000, Text by Majorie Dorner
© 1992, 2000, Cover and interior art by Allan Servoss
All rights reserved. Except for brief quotations in critical articles or reviews, no part of this book may be reproduced in any manner without prior written permission from the publisher:
Milkweed Editions, 1011 Washington Avenue South, Suite 300, Minneapolis, Minnesota 55415
(800) 520-6455
www.milkweed.org

Published 2000 by Milkweed Editions
Printed in the United States of America
Cover design by redletterdesign.com
Cover and interior art by Allan Servoss
Interior design by R. W. Scholes
The text of this book is set in Caslon 76.

00 01 02 03 04   5 4 3 2 1

First Edition 2000

Milkweed Editions is nonprofit publisher. Original publication of this book was generously sponsored by the James R. Thorpe Foundation and the Elmer L. and Eleanor J. Andersen Foundation and additional support was provided by the Literature Program of the National Endowment for the Arts; Cowles Media/Star Tribune Foundation; Dayton Hudson Foundation for Dayton's and Target Stores; First Bank System Foundation; General Mills Foundation; I. A. O'Shaughnessy Foundation; Jerome Foundation; Andrew W. Mellon Foundation; Minnesota State Arts Board through an appropriation by the Minnesota Legislature; Northwest Area Foundation; and by generous individuals. We gratefully acknowledge support for the publication of this edition of the book from the Elmer L. and Eleanor J. Andersen Foundation; James Ford Bell Foundation; Bush Foundation; General Mills Foundation; Honeywell Foundation; Jerome Foundation; McKnight Foundation; Minnesota State Arts Board through an appropriation by the Minnesota State Legislature; Norwest Foundation on behalf of Norwest Bank Minnesota; Lawrence M. O'Shaughnessy Charitable Income Trust in honor of Lawrence M. O'Shaughnessy; Oswald Family Foundation; Ritz Foundation on behalf of Mr. and Mrs. E. J. Phelps Jr.; John and Beverly Rollwagen Fund of the Minneapolis Foundation; St. Paul Companies, Inc.; Star Tribune Foundation; Target Foundation on behalf of Dayton's, Mervyn's California and Target Stores; U.S. Bancorp Piper Jaffray Foundation on behalf of U.S. Bancorp Piper Jaffray; and generous individuals.

Library of Congress Cataloging-in-Publication Data

Dorner, Marjorie.
    Winter roads, summer fields / Marjorie Dorner.
      p. cm.
    ISBN 1-57131-032-0
    1. Farm life — Middle West — Fiction.   I. Title.
PS3554.0677W56 1991
813'.54—dc20   91-13673
                                CIP

For Frances Katherine Rank Dorner (1892–1982),
who gave me some of these stories—among other things.

Acknowledgments

"Pin Money," *Primavera*, Vol. 9, 1985.

"Lee Ann's Little Killing," *FallOut*, Spring/Summer, 1983.

"Mass for the Dead," *Great River Review*, Vol. 3, No. 2, 1981.

"Changeling," *New Renaissance*, No. 22, Spring, 1988.

"Winter Roads," *Mississippi Valley Review*, Vol. 14, No. 1, Fall/Winter, 1984–85.

"Last Harvest," *North Country Anvil*, No. 13, Oct-Nov, 1974.

WINTER ROADS, SUMMER FIELDS

Winter Roads, Summer Fields

HAMMERN TOWNSHIP
1935

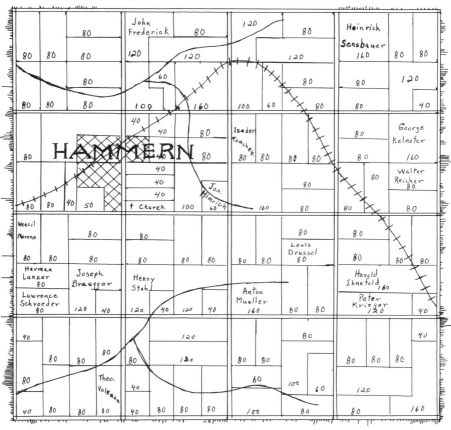

HAMMERN

John Frederick

Heinrich Sensbauer

Isador Tomchek

George Kelnofer

Walter Reicher

Jos. Hinrich

† Church

Wencil Merens

Louis Drussel

Herman Lanzer

Joseph Braegger

Henry Stahl

Anton Mueller

Harold Ihnefeld

Lawrence Schroeder

Peter Krieger

Theo. Volkman

80 80 80 80 120 80 80 160 80 80 120 120 120 120 160 120 120 160 80 80 60 60 80 120 80 80 80 100 160 100 60 80 80 40 40 40 80 80 80 160 80 40 40 80 80 40 40 80 80 80 80 40 50 100 60 160 80 80 80 80 80 80 80 80 80 80 80 80 80 80 80 80 80 80 80 80 80 80 80 80 80 160 80 120 40 120 40 120 40 160 80 80 120 40 40 80 120 80 120 80 80 80 80 80 80 80 40 80 80 80 40 120 80 80 60 100 60 120 40 80 80 40 100 80 80 160

HAMMERN TOWNSHIP
1992

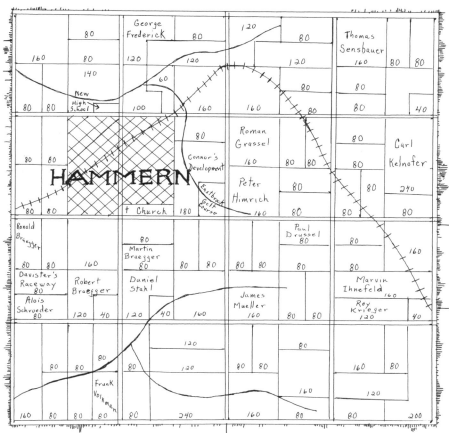

HAMMERN

George Frederick

Thomas Sensbauer

New High School

Roman Grassel

Connor's Development

Peter Himrich

Eastbrook Golf Course

† Church

Curl Kelnofer

Carl Kelnofer

Ronald Braegger

Paul Drussel

Martin Braegger

Davister's Raceway

Robert Braegger

Daniel Stahl

James Mueller

Marvin Ihnefeld

Alois Schvoeder

Roy Krieger

Frank Volkman

80 160 80 120 120 80 80 Thomas Sensbauer
160 80 120 120 120 160 80 80
140 60 80 80
80 80 100 160 160 80 80 40
80 160
80 80 160 80 80 80 240
80 80 180 80 80 80
80 160 80
80 80 160 80 80 80 80 80 80
80 80 160
120 40 120 40 160 160 80 80 120 40
120 80
80 80 80 80 120 80 160 80
160 80
160 80 80 80 80 240 160 80 80 200

Love's Mansion

(1935)

Celie turned sideways on the worn bench and looked at Marty Braegger as if she had never seen him before. She couldn't imagine what had happened to make him look and act this way. He sat on the other end of the bench, intently examining the toes of his shoes, his Sunday shoes, which made up only one end of the transformation in his appearance. His coppery hair, which usually stood out from his head like a brush, was parted and combed flat with something that made it look wet, and he had on a suit that Celie had seen him wear only in church. Except to wave away an occasional fly, he kept his hands between his knees, and he didn't lift his head when he spoke to her either. Not that he talked much, and this was the oddest change of all. Marty was usually full of talk, joking and teasing all the time.

Celie had known Marty all her life, for the Braeggers lived on the next farm down the road. In the past few years, he had grown from a scrawny, impish little boy into a tall, lively seventeen-year-old. But Celie hadn't really paid him much attention. It was his sisters who mattered to her, Marty's younger sisters. Among them, Celie felt plain and awkward, for they were vivid children with sparkling faces and pealing laughs, but they were good-natured and generous, pulling the quieter Celie into the bright world of their activities. Elaine was fifteen, the same age as Celie, Hannah was fourteen, and Angeline was twelve. The other two girls and the twin boys were too young to count for much, except to take a part when the girls played house.

The Braegger house seemed to Celie to have a circle of light around it, even though it was just an ordinary farmhouse that Joe Braegger, the father, had built with his own hands and had added on to over the years as the family grew. It was a house filled with noise, not a very tidy place, but everybody seemed happy there.

Celie liked Joe and Kate Braegger and secretly wished that they were *her* parents. Joe was a big, dark-haired man who laughed loudly and teased people to show that he liked them. Kate was larger than Celie's own mother, though not at all fat—a tall, merry woman who always said things like "Let's roll up our sleeves here and all pitch in." Celie thought she was beautiful. Whenever Joe and Kate were together, they seemed to talk just by looking at each other, and there was something between them that made Celie feel warm just being in the room with them. She spent as much time at the Braeggers' house as her mother would let her, but the Braegger girls never played at Celie's house. Somehow, without even speaking, Celie's mother made it seem that giggling and practical jokes and dressing up were bad, something to be ashamed of.

So it had seemed odd, this late June evening, when Celie's father had come back from driving her mother to the church card party in Hammern and had told Celie that Marty was coming over to visit with her.

"Why don't you brush your hair and put on a nice dress, Cecelia?" he'd said. Her father was the only person who called her Cecelia. Her mother said "Cecelia Anna Lanzer" when she was angry, but when Pa said her name it sounded nice. He was a quiet man who looked like he could never get over being sad though he was trying. He was sometimes a little rough in his speech, but he was never really unkind. So Celie didn't ask him why she should get dressed up for Marty Braegger; she just went upstairs and put on her yellow eyelet blouse and her light blue jumper. She brushed her pale hair into a rope down her back and gave her angular body a brief glance in the hall mirror.

It was a warm, rather humid night, so she'd asked Marty onto the side porch where the old bench was nailed against the outside wall. Pa had gone down to the barn where a heifer was in labor with her first calf; he always took these heifers inside when their time was near so he could help if the birth was hard. Celie had often watched the calves being born. Now she sat here puzzling

Winter Roads, Summer Fields

about why Marty had come over and why he seemed unable to make his tongue work, except in short questions.

"You ever learn to dance?" he mumbled to his clasped hands.

"Well, Elaine and Hannah and me sometimes pretend about dancing," she said, "but there's no music."

"You like it?"

"I'm not very good. I'm clumsy, I guess. 'Goose Legs' is what your pa calls me."

Ordinarily, Marty would have chuckled at this reminder; now his brow puckered into a deep frown.

"Pa teases too much, sometimes," he said.

After a long pause, he glanced quickly at Celie and then away again.

"I'm not much at dancing either, I guess, but I suppose we gotta do it sometime. People go to kermisses and such things, and there's always dancing. Matt Mueller is getting married next week, and there'll be a dance."

Encouraged by this rather long speech, Celie picked up what she thought was the subject Marty wanted to discuss.

"Nick didn't have a dance at his wedding last month," she said, referring to her own brother, "so I guess dancing might not be something you just *have* to learn."

"Oh, it's not that." In the half-light from the window behind him, he looked as if he might be blushing. "I'm trying to learn. My pa is a good dancer, and he says that I'm getting better. I'm actually getting to think it might be fun."

"I see," she murmured, but she didn't. She again felt at a loss, unable to tell what her part was supposed to be. But Celie never expressed impatience or boredom; she just waited quietly for things to become clear.

Marty moved the toe of his shoe back and forth across a knothole in the porch floor and then looked out toward the moon before he spoke again.

"I'm thinking I might try to do some dancing at Matt's wedding."

"We're not invited to that wedding," Celie said. "Mama says the Muellers are kinda stuck-up."

He looked back at her, his face momentarily restored to the Marty she knew.

"Oh, no, they're not," he snorted. "We're some kinda shirttail relation to them, that's all. They got so many folks, they can't invite nobody except relatives."

"I see," she said.

"You could go to that wedding dance if you went with me," Marty said, looking at the lapels of his jacket.

Celie sat staring at him, her breath held in, her mind temporarily numb. Marty Braegger was asking her out, was meaning to court her. When she'd let the air out of her lungs and breathed again, she realized that her father must have known about this, that Marty must have asked him about it first. She felt her cheeks burning. She was not ready for this, had never thought about Marty as anything other than Elaine and Hannah's big brother. He was almost like her own big brother, except that he was nicer to her than Nick had ever been. She'd only just finished school; she still played with her dolls sometimes, when she was alone in her room.

Marty had glanced at her several times, out of the corners of his eyes, but now he looked out across the yard. His ear, the one Celie could see in the light from the window, was very red. She knew she should say something, but now words had left her completely. She had no idea what girls were supposed to say under these circumstances. Elaine said that she sometimes danced with boys at coin showers, but Celie had never seen Elaine with a boy and only half-believed her anyway, so there was nothing for Celie to imitate. Her mother had never told her about her own courtship, never spoke about such things at all.

It seemed that the silence had gone on for hours since the last time Marty had spoken. When Celie heard the sound of her father's shoes on the porch steps, she was so startled that she let out a muffled scream and sprang up from the bench.

"I'm sorry to disturb you," Pa said, very formal, as if he were talking to strangers. "I wouldn't do it otherwise, but I got trouble down in the barn."

"What kind of trouble?" Marty asked, standing up.

"The calf is coming breech," Pa said. "The heifer is never gonna make it. We gotta do something, or I'll lose 'em both."

"You gonna get the vet?"

"I couldn't pay him," Pa said, and he looked even sadder than usual.

"It's this depression," Marty said, and he looked embarrassed. "Money's short for everybody."

"Maybe we can save 'em if we work together," Celie's pa said. "Are you willing to give it a try?"

"Sure," Marty said. "I've helped my pa pull calves out when it was needed."

"We gotta be quick about it. You'll have to get out of those clothes." Then he turned to Celie, who was standing back against the house, quiet and listening. "Get Marty some of Nick's old clothes, will you, Cecelia? Maybe you can come along to hold the light."

"I'll have to change too," she said, looking down at the porch.

"Okay, but hurry it up. The heifer is down and she's pushing real hard. She's already done herself some damage, I think."

Celie led the way up to Nick's room with Marty plodding silently behind. The room smelled musty from being closed up in the summer. Nick was living with his new wife's family and said there was no room for all of his clothes; shirts and trousers were still folded neatly in the old chest of drawers that had once belonged to Grandma Merens. Celie pulled out some overalls and a white, short-sleeved shirt.

"Here," she said softly and dropped the clothes onto the yellowed chenille bedspread.

Marty just stood there with his hands in his pockets, staring at the clothes, while Celie walked quickly past him and into her own room next door. Going into Nick's room had started her thinking about her brother and his recent marriage. There hadn't been much warning that he actually wanted to marry Loretta Duescher, but in April Celie's mother had told her she would be a bridesmaid. Celie still didn't understand why her mother had seemed so angry about the whole wedding business, so tight-lipped and weepy. And Pa had grown even more quiet and sad. Maybe they just didn't like Loretta and that was why the wedding was so small—Celie was the *only* bridesmaid—and why there was no dance. In fact, everybody at the wedding had seemed pretty sad, especially Loretta. Nick had never talked much to Celie; he was four years older and considered girls pretty sorry, anyway. So she hadn't mentioned his marriage to anybody, not even to the Braegger girls. Still, the house seemed even quieter and more empty without Nick clomping up and down the stairs. Celie wondered what it was like for him in the Dueschers' house.

While she thought about Nick, Celie automatically stripped off her jumper and blouse and stepped out of her shoes. She was reaching for her overalls when she heard sounds coming from the other side of the wall, faint sounds of rustling fabric and clinking buckles. Her face began to burn again, remembering. Marty Braegger had asked her to a dance. Marty Braegger was taking his clothes off in the next room, just a few feet away from her. She stood still, holding her breath, imagining the shirt coming off his long, thin arms, the Sunday trousers going down over his legs. She could picture his long body bending over to pull the trousers off over his feet. Maybe he had no undershirt on beneath his suit—it was a warm night. Celie felt a little faint from not breathing, and her face felt hot.

Now there were no sounds coming from behind the wall, and she started a little, thinking that maybe he was listening too, listening for any sounds from her room; maybe he was thinking about her undressing too, so close to him. Celie looked down at her underwear, at the sleeveless vest covering her small breasts and the simple cotton panties. Then she snatched up her work shirt and flung it onto her arms, breathing quickly now, almost in a panic. She pulled her overalls on and then ran downstairs to the kitchen where her barn shoes stood next to the back door. She waited for Marty on the porch, her arms folded tightly across her chest.

When he came outside, he looked more like himself again. Partly this was the clothes, and partly it was that he had messed his hair while changing. They walked together to the barn without speaking.

The barn was as familiar to Celie as her house was; she would have needed no light to find her way around even on a dark night. The stalls where Pa kept the heifers were just to the left of the door, and the alley stretched away to the right, empty stanchions on either side of it. The smells of cows and straw bedding and hay and ground oats blended into a medley that Celie never even consciously noticed anymore. She spent some part of every day in the barn, helping with milking, running the cream separator, scrubbing the milk cans. Her mother took care of the house chores and seldom came into the barn.

Inside the first of the two stalls, Celie and Marty could see the heifer lying on her left side, her stomach bulging upward. For a moment she seemed almost dead, but then her side heaved and she lifted her head from the straw. Celie's father was standing at the front of the stall; he had made a rope halter and fitted it over the young cow's head.

"We have to get her up," he said. "If she stands, the calf will slide back down into her belly where we can move it around."

Marty went inside the stall and around behind the heifer. Celie's father pulled on the halter and began shouting at the downed animal.

"Come on, girl, get up! Get on your feet."

Marty shoved from the side, bent into a crouch so that he could reach under the heifer's neck and front shoulders. The animal struggled to get her front knees under herself, but she got no further, the weight of her hindquarters holding her in the straw.

"Come on!" Pa was really yelling now. "You're not gonna die

down there, damn it!" And he leaned back with all his weight, stretching the heifer's neck upward.

Marty turned around and put his back against the cow's side. Bracing his legs against the back of the stall, he pushed with his shoulders and upper back.

"Doesn't that hurt her?" Celie asked, her eyes wide and staring.

"Hurt her?" Pa snarled, his breath coming between clenched teeth. "She'll do worse than hurt if we can't get her up."

The heifer's back legs kicked a few times, sending straw flying over Celie's shoes. At last the cow got her hooves against the floor, heaved her body over, and scrambled up. Her belly swung beneath her.

"All right, all right," Pa gasped. "Let's get her right side against the wall over here. You'll have to keep her standing, Marty, while I get that calf's legs straightened out."

He and Marty shouldered the heifer against the wall, and Marty leaned into her side to hold her there. Celie's father hurried behind the animal and lifted her tail.

"Bring that light closer, Celie," he said. "If you climb up on the gate there, you can lean over with it."

Celie stepped up onto the second rail of the gate, her stomach braced against the top rail, and leaned into the stall with the lantern stretched out toward her father. Marty made a groaning sound as the cow swayed toward him and began to sag at the knees.

"Christ!" Pa shouted. "Keep her up!"

He sprang around to help Marty, and the two of them shoved the heifer upright again.

"I'll have to hold her," Pa said. "She'll listen to me."

He was breathing hard, as if he had been running for a long time.

"You'll have to straighten the calf out, Marty."

Marty just looked at him for a second, and Celie could see his hazel eyes widening, his forehead puckering.

"Just do what I tell you, boy." Pa had lost patience as well as breath. "I'll tell you what to do."

Marty moved behind the heifer.

"Just reach inside," Pa said. "You'll find the calf's backside. That's what's wrong here. The back legs are folded under the calf, and what you gotta do is reach under the little bugger and find the back feet. The idea is to get 'em out from under him so you can pull 'em out first, before the rear end. After that, she can fall over if she wants to. We can help her get the calf out then."

Marty closed and opened his right hand just once and then plunged it into the swollen opening under the heifer's tail. Celie held the lantern forward, the top of the gate pressing up under her ribs.

"I can feel the tail," Marty said.

"Well, you gotta get under that to the legs," Pa grunted, leaning with all his strength against the heifer.

Marty pushed his arm further inside. In the light from the lantern, Celie could see the pale hair glistening on his upper forearm before it disappeared inside the animal. She closed her eyes and swallowed hard, her left hand gripping the post above the gate hinges.

"I found the legs," Marty said, his voice muffled as he turned his head away from Celie.

"Get down to the feet," Pa said. "Fast! She doesn't like this, and I don't know how long I can hold her up."

When Celie opened her eyes, Marty's arm had disappeared almost up to his shoulder and he was straining forward, his left hand bracing against the cow's flank.

"I got one," Marty said. "There's the other one too."

He began to withdraw his arm. Celie could see the sleeve of her brother's shirt coming away from the animal's body. It was stained with a bright half-moon of blood. When Marty's upper arm became visible, that too was wet and streaked with blood. The heifer lurched and made a deep moaning sound.

"Damn!" Marty cried. "Lost 'em." And his arm slid back inside the cow.

Celie felt she couldn't breathe anymore, felt that there was no air left in the barn. She turned her face away and lifted her head to try to breathe and to swallow her nausea. In the next stall, where Celie's gaze fell, there was another heifer, one Pa had brought inside because she was almost ready to have her calf. The animal stood quietly, calmly chewing. Her bloated belly hung beneath her, plumping her sides so that her midsection looked like a barrel.

"I've got the feet again," Marty was saying behind Celie's head, but she didn't turn around. The heifer she was watching suddenly lifted her tail and sent a stream of urine out across the straw bedding in her stall. Steam rose from the straw, and the acrid smell sprang almost immediately into Celie's nose.

She felt she was choking, her throat closing in a spasm of sickness. Her head felt light and empty, and when she closed her eyes bursts of red light appeared on the insides of her eyelids.

"Hold that light steady, Celie," her father snapped. "We almost got this calf out here."

Celie turned back to them, but she couldn't look. She just hung the lantern over the gatepost and made her legs move to lower herself from the rail. Still shaking, she found her way toward the barn door like a blind person, running her hand along the rough wood to guide herself. Behind her, her father was calling, "Celie! What the hell? Celie!" But she never turned back.

Inside the house, Celie went straight to the little spare bedroom next to the cookstove. It was used only when someone in the house was sick and needed to be close to the warmth of the stove. It was also the only room in the house with a door that locked. Celie closed herself inside and slid the bolt. Her legs were shaking, and she had to swallow over and over to keep from vomiting. After bending over the back of the narrow cot for a few minutes, she sat down, the rusted springs creaking under her weight.

She was remembering something she had kept herself from

Winter Roads, Summer Fields

thinking about for many years. She'd remembered it in the barn but had sent it so quickly out of her mind that everything else seemed to go with it, leaving her head hollow, light, emptied of everything except the impulse to flee.

The summer Celie was eight years old had been a particularly hot, sticky summer—people still talked about the summer of '28. Grandma Merens was still alive then and living in the old house across the road with Aunt Polly. Celie's parents had a summer kitchen out in the backyard where the stove's heat couldn't make the big house any more unbearably hot than it already was. All that summer, Grandma Merens had come over to take her weekly baths at Celie's house, where the bathwater could be heated in the summer kitchen, and where Pa was on hand to carry the steaming copper boiler into the house for her.

One Saturday evening in August, Celie's parents had gone into the backyard to catch the breeze from the northeast, and Celie had wandered around to the front of the house where the wind was making the kitchen window shade flap against the screen. She knew that Grandma Merens was inside taking a bath and was drawn to the window to see if she could get a look at her. Celie had never seen any adult without clothes on.

By crouching down against the house with her eyes just above the window ledge, Celie could get a glimpse of the inside of the kitchen every time the shade flapped. For a while, all she saw was her grandmother's back, wide and white, with the washcloth going up and down along one arm and then the other. But, at last, Grandma Merens stood up, grasping the sides of the metal tub and heaving herself upright. Before the shade fell down, Celie caught a glimpse of her grandmother's pale, sagging buttocks. By the time the shade flapped inward again, Grandma had turned toward the window, and Celie was looking straight at her immense, distended stomach, stretch marks scarring its sides, and below it a stark triangle of dark hair.

"I'm telling." The voice was almost against her ear, and Celie fell over sideways from the shock. Nick had crept up behind her, noiseless as a spider in the soft grass.

And he did tell, almost immediately. Celie's mother found her behind her bed, crouching against the wall. She pulled Celie upright, her lean, harsh face bending toward the child to look once into Celie's eyes. Then she began to slap the child, first in the face and then, when she ducked, on the top of her head and the back of her neck. All the while, she kept hissing over and over, "You dirty girl. You dirty, dirty little girl."

Years later, when hair began to grow between Celie's legs, she was too afraid to look down at herself, dressed and undressed in the dark. And she never asked why her mother insisted that she bind her breasts for the first two years after they'd begun to grow. She had quit binding them only last winter when Pa said that she must stop, that it was unhealthy. But she didn't ask why it should be unhealthy, either; she just stopped wearing the cloth wrap. She never asked questions at all.

But in the barn, she had remembered. There, between the two heifers, she'd remembered about Grandma Merens in the bath, and at the same time, all at once, before she could drive it from her mind, she'd realized that this was the way women had their babies too. They were courted and got married so that they could have babies in this way, swelling up like the women she sometimes saw in church, and then having babies dragged from between their legs in blood and slime.

Celie sagged down onto the cot, burying her mouth in the stale-smelling pillowcase, her stomach knotting. Grandma Merens and her own mother—they'd had babies like that. And Kate Braegger. Even Kate Braegger—eight times. It was awful, more awful than anything Celie had ever thought about. She wanted to cry, but there were no tears, only the burning in her face and the taste of nausea in her mouth.

Later, she heard her father and Marty come into the house, heard Marty go upstairs. After a few minutes, she heard her father's voice on the other side of the door.

"Cecelia? Are you in there?" He turned the knob only once.

"Yes," she said tonelessly.

"The calf's fine. It's a bull calf."

Celie said nothing.

"What's wrong with you, Cecelia? You've seen calves born before." And now she could hear him thumping softly on the door. "Aren't you coming out to say good-bye to Marty? He done us a big favor tonight."

How could she make him understand that she would never be able to look at Marty Braegger again?

"No," she said and put her face back into the pillow.

Her father went away from the door, and then Celie could hear him talking to Marty, who'd come back downstairs.

"I'm sorry about your shoes," Pa said.

"Oh, that's all right," Marty said. "I can clean them up when I get home."

They went outside, so Celie couldn't hear them anymore. After a while, she stood up and moved to the high, narrow window that looked out toward the road. A little breeze was coming through the screen, and Celie drew in two long breaths. She watched Marty walking toward his home, watched him until his red hair, which seemed to catch the moonlight, disappeared behind the hill.

Herbert

(1948)

In the summer of 1948, Matt Mueller decided that his son Jim, who had turned twelve in March, was ready to become a full member of the threshing crew. The boy had worked hard shocking up the oats, could drive a tractor like a man, and seldom grumbled about his work. They talked about it one hot night, though it was Matt who did most of the talking.

Jim wanted to work with the field crew, out with the horses in the open air, but his father thought he wasn't strong enough yet to be a bundle pitcher, and the men who brought their wagons would drive their own teams. So he was to be on the yard crew, but again he was not ready to be an unloader or a bag carrier—the full-grown men could do this back-breaking work all day, and Jim might get in their way.

"You can level grain after it's dumped upstairs," his father said. "You'll be working with Herbert Servy. He used to do it between loads, but we've got a bigger crew this year, so he'll mostly carry bags. He'll come up between loads to give you a hand, though. You can kinda keep an eye on him for me. I always worry he'll slide into the grain bin and suffocate. I don't think he'd have the sense to get out by himself."

The boy wasn't pleased. The closed-in upper floor of the granary would become almost unbearable as the men dumped bag after bag of fresh oats onto the floor, sending clouds of dust back and forth in the stale air. And working with Herbert! Jim could never think about Herbert without thinking of his eyes. As a young child, Jim had thought that those eyes looked exactly like marbles, like the blue marbles whose transparent surfaces showed planes and flecks of color inside. In those years, Jim had believed that Herbert was a special being called into existence only for the few days every summer when the threshing crew came to the farm.

Surely so odd a creature just disappeared into smoke for the rest of the year. Only when he got a little older did Jim begin to see that Herbert's oddness made him an easy target. Maybe, he thought now, working with Herbert would make a target of him too. But he was glad to be on the crew, recognized his rookie status, and so kept silent.

The gathering of the crew on that first morning of the harvest seemed brand-new to the boy, as if he'd never seen it before. The horses made their harnesses rattle and creak as they nibbled on the dew-soaked grass along the east fence. The men stood in groups of two or three with their arms folded inside their overall bibs. Jim stood among them, imitating this gesture, for his great ambition in life at this age was to be just like his father, his uncles, his older cousins. Pa had brought in the threshing machine the night before, pulling it with the Ten-twenty which would now provide the power to run it. It sat under the open doors of the mow, its dragon-like head toward the granary, its straw-blower aimed into the mow.

Breakfast was already spread out on the long table behind the house. Jim and his father had set up the table that morning before milking; it was just planks laid across three sawhorses and then covered with an oilcloth. Grandma and Aunt Hilda had arrived before dawn; they would help his mother with the cooking and with the evening milking for as long as it took to get the grain in. When Grandma came out of the house with two enamel coffee pots, it was a signal for the men to approach the table.

Herbert had not arrived. Breakfast was almost over when he came, walking in from the east. Everyone else had arrived on some vehicle, either riding on the empty wagons or in their own cars, which were now parked on the south driveway to be out of the way. The men at the table began laughing as soon as they caught sight of Herbert. He walked at a forward angle, as if his tall frame had to lean into the air to push it out of his way. He began to wave as soon as he saw that they were watching him, and he broke into a clumsy trot.

"Come on, Herbert," the men shouted. "Get a move on. There won't be any food left."

When he reached them, he was grinning broadly and shouting, "Save me some. Save me some." Despite the fact that it was the middle of summer, he wore a flannel shirt and woolen dress trousers held up by suspenders.

"How come you're so late, Herbert?" This from Philip Mueller, Pa's first cousin, who'd been in the army and was sure he knew a lot.

"Ain't no alarm clock in the barn," Herbert said around a mouthful of bread. "Tomorrow I'll be first." This was because he would sleep in the Muellers' barn until the harvest was over. His clothes were already covered with dust and bits of straw. His hair, the color almost indistinguishable from the straw, was matted in the back, sticking straight out on the top and sides. Reddish beard stubble covered his huge lower jaw, and the extraordinary eyes seemed to be the only clean patches on his face. He held his eyes open so wide that the white showed all around the pale blue irises; it made him look constantly surprised and a little wild, like a skittish horse. His front teeth had a space between them through which he was now sucking coffee, and they always showed slightly under his upper lip. It was not really possible to guess his age. To the boy he looked old, as all adults did. To the men he seemed young; they were used to treating him like a child, so it was easier to think of him as young. He might have been in his early thirties; he might have been forty-five.

"Well, let's get goin'," Pa said, and the men got up from the table. There were thirteen in all, counting the boy. Uncle Peter took his sons Cyril and Jake and the Tomchek boys, Wencil (who was called Jim) and George, out for the first load. The Tomchek wagon, with old Isador driving, would follow in a half hour, and Pa would take out his own wagon as Peter's wagon was being unloaded. The field crew would take turns pitching bundles into the wagon and leveling the load on top.

As the men moved away from the table, Jim heard Philip say

to Carl Bergmann, "Shit. I put salt in his coffee and he didn't even notice it." The boy didn't have to wonder who Carl meant; he chuckled along with his cousin and his cousin's friend as they went down the hill toward the still-silent machines. Behind them, Herbert was talking loudly to the boy's mother, who'd looked daggers at Philip when he said that about the coffee. She didn't approve of such "funning," Jim knew. Last year, when he'd mocked little Willy Reicher who still sucked his thumb in the first grade, his mother had said, "You stop that. You could be nicer to him, you know, because I don't think that child gets much niceness at home."

Before the first day was half over, they'd all fallen into the rhythms of the harvest. When a full wagon would pull up to the threshing machine's two-story-high mouth, the driver would water the horses while Louie Drussel, a neighboring farmer, would scramble up to begin feeding the bundles, head first, into the machine's slashing teeth that shredded straw and twine into a fine chaff that would provide bedding for the cows all winter long. The vibrating sieves at the maw of the great machine caught the grain, shook it free of the straw, and moved it along past the blowers. Here, the straw was blown upwards into the mow where John, Peter's youngest son, waded into the choking dust with a pitchfork to level the bright mounds. The oats went onto conveyer belts and finally spilled from spouts on the machine's sides into empty bags.

Philip, Carl, and Herbert were bag carriers. As a bag was nearly filled, one of them would pull a lever to move the flowing grain onto the other belt and into an empty bag suspended from the alternate spout. He would then lift the full bag off its hooks, close the opening with one twist, shoulder the bag, and carry it up twelve steps to the granary door. By the time he'd dumped the oats inside, another bag was filled and coming up the stairs.

Inside the granary, Jim wielded a large shovel, the cleanest shovel he'd ever used, to move the grain into the bin, a large rectangular hole in the center of the floor from which a steel funnel extended down to the first floor, ending in a trapdoored spout

Winter Roads, Summer Fields

small enough to fit into a burlap bag. From the first floor, the grain could be bagged again for the weekly trips to the mill. When the bin was full, the boy used the shovel like a snowplow to spread the heaps of grain over the floor and towards the outer walls. All the yard work was done in an almost deafening roar of machinery.

Between loads, someone would throttle down the tractor to a grumbling throb, and the crew would move out of the dust clouds to stretch out on the back lawn. John and Jim could come outside if they were caught up. If Jim didn't appear, Herbert would sprint up the steps, take the shovel from the boy's blistering hands, and dispatch the mounds of oats in a few minutes. Just before lunch, there was a lull between loads long enough to bring all the yard crew onto the grass for a rest.

"Jimmy," Philip said. "Get me a drink of water."

Stung, the boy remained silent. He didn't move.

"Well," Philip said, sitting up to look at the boy. "You gonna go?"

"I'm not carrying water this year," the boy managed to say. This had been his job in previous years and was considered a job for a child.

Louie Drussel made a sudden snorting sound and Philip's eyes narrowed.

"I'll get it," Herbert said, jumping up.

Philip and Carl exchanged a look.

"Let's go together," Philip said with all his teeth showing.

Carl got up to join them, but Louie stretched a little flatter into the grass. Jim wanted to watch, though, so he followed the three men.

"You go first, Herbert," Carl said, lifting the pump handle.

Herbert looked at Philip as if for permission and then, seeing only a smile, cupped his hands and bent forward. Philip shoved the big man hard so that he landed with his chest in the muddy water under the pump's spout. Carl was pumping hard now and the cold water splashed all over Herbert's head and shoulders. He rolled over, but increased water pressure sent an icy stream straight into his face. He came up sputtering and shaking his big head. Carl was howling and Philip kept making a wheezing noise that sounded like "Hee, hee, hee."

Herbert threw both of his arms straight out from his sides in a movement so sudden that both of the other men stopped laughing and jumped away from him. Then he grinned, a gaping smile that cut across the dust and mud under his eyes. "Great!" he shouted. "That feels great. I'm not hot anymore. I'll pump for you if you wanna do it." He looked at Carl and Philip, his eyes happy like a child's. "Come on, I'll pump." His glee was contagious, and Jim started to laugh again.

"That's okay, Herbert," Carl said. "A drink's all I want."

At lunch, the boy's father asked, "Why's Herbert wet?"

"Maybe he figured he needed a bath," Philip said.

Pa scowled at his younger cousin. "I don't want any horsin' around."

"Naw. No horsin' around."

After lunch, Jim began to notice that Herbert was appearing with bags of oats more often than he had in the morning. The boy stepped into the doorway to watch. Through clouds of dust, he saw Carl lifting a full bag onto Herbert's shoulder and, above the noise, he could hear Philip shouting, "Now you run, Herbert. Hurry up!" And Herbert actually did manage to run up the stairs with his load, flashing a grin at the boy in the doorway. At the machine below, Carl had switched spouts and Philip was shouldering a bag. By the time Herbert got down again, the other bag was ready for him. He was carrying every second bag, while Carl and Philip took turns on the alternate. The two friends shouted encouragement to Herbert and smiled at Jim. The boy grinned, mopped the sweat off his own face with his sleeve, and went back inside with his shovel.

At the afternoon break, when they'd all gathered at the table in the shade to munch on sandwiches and drink lemonade, Herbert came up to Jim and bent his great jaw to the boy's ear.

"I'm way ahead, you know," he whispered.

"Ahead? Ahead of what?" The boy hadn't bothered to whisper, feeling nervous that the others would think he had secrets with Herbert. The big man shushed him, looking around conspiratorially.

"Ahead of those guys. I'm carrying lots more bags than them, ain't I?"

The boy felt a flash of irritation. To be teased and tricked and not even know it!

"You know, Herbert," he said very seriously, "you ought to give those guys a chance."

"What?"

"Well, you're lots bigger and stronger than they are, so you're bound to win. Wouldn't it be fair to give them a chance to catch up?"

Herbert had begun to look very worried halfway through this speech.

"You really think so?"

"Yes, Herbert, I really think so."

"I suppose. Yeah, you're right. I'll be good." And he was grinning again.

For the rest of the afternoon, Jim would duck outside every now and then to watch. Carl and Philip would still be shouting, "Come on, Herbert. Grab this bag. The other one's almost full," and Herbert would spread his big arms as if he were fighting off an attack, bellowing, "Naw, that's all right. You can take it. I don't mind." Sometimes, the bags would run over while this dialogue was going on, spilling grain onto the graveled yard. Jim smiled to himself, knowing Philip was going to catch it from Pa.

That night, the boy was so exhausted that he fell asleep immediately, despite the pain in his hands, and without once thinking about the man who slept in the straw that the day's labor had put into the barn.

In the middle of the next morning, there was a long break between loads, and Herbert came up into the granary to heap the growing piles of oats against the far wall. The boy shooed some curious cats back out the door and then sat on the stairs to get some air. Carl, Philip, Louie, and John had gone to the pump for a drink. In a few minutes, Herbert flopped down next to the boy.

"Ma told me not to feed 'em the strainer pads," he said.

"What? Feed what the strainer pads?"

"The cats. Pa said never to feed cats at all cuz they's supposed to find their own food—eat mice and stuff. But I liked to feed 'em, 'specially the little ones. When I cleaned the milk strainer, I'd just pour the leavin's in a pan. But those little beelers ate the strainer pads too. They liked 'em and I thought it must be all right."

"What happened?"

"Well, sometimes they'd walk around with pieces of strainer pad hangin' out their asses, just like another tail. That's how Ma found out. She made me stop doin' it, but she didn't tell Pa on me. She knew I didn't mean to hurt 'em."

"Did they die from it?"

"Not's I know. Some of 'em died, but cats get distemper a lot so it was hard to tell. They was cute little beelers too, and I used to bawl when I found 'em dead. You got any pets?"

The boy thought for a moment.

"Trixie, I suppose. She's a good cow dog, but I don't know that Pa would like to call her a pet."

There was a pause; then the boy said, "Does your Ma still tease you about those cats?"

The blue eyes looked confused for a second.

"Oh, Ma's dead a long time now. Pa, too. She was pretty old when she had me, and *that* was a long time ago."

"You live on the home place alone?"

"Ain't no home place now. I live all over. I like it. In the winter, though, I live in the city with Esther."

"Who's Esther?"

"My sister. She's pretty old too. She don't like me and I don't like her."

"Why do you live with her then?"

"Can't live outside in the winter. Tried it once, but I had to go to the hospital after a while."

Without warning, he pulled off his right shoe—it hadn't been laced—and pointed at the scarred stumps at the end of his foot. He looked almost proud.

"Lost them toes. Now I go to Esther's."

The boy swallowed several times, and then Herbert put his shoe back on.

"How old are you, Herbert?"

The big man's face got the worried look again.

"Don't know. Ma used to tell me. Esther knows but she don't say. Jeez, I hate that city."

Almost automatically, the boy turned his face in the direction of his own house, even though the corner of the granary made it impossible to see the comfortable homestead where three generations of Muellers had lived. Into the silence, the sounds of Isador Tomchek's wagon began to intrude. The rest of the crew was coming back down the hill. Herbert and Jim stood up.

"I guess them mice gotta eat too," Herbert said.

"What mice?"

"The ones that come in the barns where I sleep. They come in more when the cold weather starts. Folks don't like 'em to be in there, but I never tell on 'em."

All that day, Philip and Carl were subdued. Pa had been very angry about the spilled grain. That night, when everyone else had left, Jim asked his father for an old razor and some soap, and his mother let him have one of her clean dust rags. He took these things to Herbert and held a mirror while the big man scraped at his oversized jaw. He had to lean up close to the mirror because it was getting dark outside. When he finished, there was a little film of lather on the puddle under the pump.

On the third day, there was only a half-day's work left, no more than six loads. The weather had held and the harvest was big, so Matt decided to set up some beer; it was both a celebration and a way to pay the crew. Herbert, Carl, and Philip would actually receive wages. Other crew members had farms too, so they worked for Pa in exchange for his labor when their harvests were ready. But Isador and Uncle Peter had grown sons to bring with them on a crew, and Pa had only Jim, so the beer was a way of evening things out. It was in a wooden barrel, lashed around with iron bands. The men who brought it had to help Pa put the barrel inside the biggest washtub in the basement. Then Pa filled the tub with cold well water. If the outside trapdoor stayed down, the basement was always dark and cool, even in summer.

Before dawn while they were milking, Pa said to Jim, "I suppose some of the yard crew will be sneaking up to the house for a few beers during the morning. You keep an eye on Herbert and see to it that he doesn't have any beer."

"Jeez. I have to watch him so he doesn't drown in the grain bin, and now I have to keep him from drinking beer. How come those other guys can drink?"

"They can handle it. Herbert would probably fall into the thresh machine."

The crew made a leisurely start to its half-day, the first wagon going out at about eight-thirty. Jim suspected that Cy and Jake had already had some beer for breakfast before they scrambled onto the Tomchek wagon. The Tomchek boys, who looked exactly alike despite the two years' difference in their ages, never talked much and seldom called attention to themselves, so it was hard to tell if they would sneak into the basement for beer, but Jim knew his cousins well enough to believe that they would. Carl and Philip waited only until Pa's wagon was out of sight behind the barn. They soon persuaded Louie to join them on their frequent trips to the back of the house.

The boy did his own work slowly, not only because his hands were almost raw by now, but so that he could call for Herbert's help between loads, to keep him from noticing where the others were going. Looking even more boyish without his stubble, Herbert would bound up the steps and send the oats flying; the heaps of grain against the walls were almost up to the ceiling by now. By the time Jim and Herbert were ready to go to the pump for a drink of water, the others would be coming back down from the house. Even John, who was only sixteen, had joined them and was beginning to look very red in the face by ten-thirty.

When the fourth load was finished, Isador unhitched his team and joined the others in the basement. Jim and Herbert shoveled grain.

"Let's get a drink," Herbert said when they were done.

"I'm not thirsty," the boy said, stalling. The others were still at the house. He stood in the doorway, rubbing his aching shoulders against the frame and scowling out into the midday sunshine. The dust against his skin felt like sand.

"Hey, watch me," Herbert shouted.

The boy turned back into the dusty gloom of the granary. The big man was hopping on one foot around the raised rim of the grain bin.

"Hey, cut that out," the boy said, alarmed. "Quit it. You're gonna fall in."

"Not me. I'm a real dancer."

Then, with a great whoop, the man threw himself backwards away from the bin and landed in a pile of grain, sliding a little before stopping spread-eagled, dust clouds settling again around him. Slowly, he began to move his arms up and down in the oats. Then he opened and closed his legs, making a wide trench that spread around him like a skirt, its edges crumbling as the grain rolled back down. His face grew quiet, the blue eyes shining up at the ceiling.

"The wind howled around the house all night," he said.

This time, the boy just let him talk.

"I was always scairt of the wind anyways, and this time I was wide-awake waiting so hard for morning to come. When we got up, the snow was piled real high outside. We could hardly get the barn doors open. Pa wore a scarf over his face cuz it was still blowin' like hell out there. Ma and I dug out the milk cans. Before we got half-done, she had ice on her eyes."

Jim squatted down in the doorway, listening.

"It was Christmastime. Pa said I was a bad boy and Santa Claus wouldn't bring me a sled. Said he'd bring me horse turds. I stayed awake all night cuz I was scairt it would be true. Then I had to wait till after milking to look in the front room."

"What was there?"

"Horse turds."

"Honest?"

"Yeah. In a big bowl."

"What did you do?"

"I bawled. I bawled so loud, Ma said the neighbors was gonna hear clear across the field." He looked pretty cheerful as he told about it, as if the loudness of his crying were an accomplishment.

"You didn't get a sled?"

"Yeah, I did. Pa dragged me back outside and it was in the shed. It was there all the while, he said. But I just couldn't stop bawlin'. Even when the wind died down after dinner, I didn't take the sled outside to try it. I was just plain miserable all day."

"Because your Pa tricked you like that?"

"Oh, no!" The blue eyes popped open even wider. "Pa did stuff like that all the time. I was bawlin' cuz I thought Santa Claus done it. Ma finally had to tell me it was Pa hid the sled. After that, I liked it."

"Oh," Jim said.

From the direction of the house, they heard a muffled burst of laughter, many voices laughing together. Herbert folded his arms and snuggled further down into his grain angel.

"You know," he said. "Folks don't like me to have any beer."

Jim snapped to attention, feeling his face turn red.

"You know about the beer?"

"I can smell it when Carl and Philip come down. I don't know why they think I shouldn't have it. I like beer. Do you like beer?"

"Naw, not much." He'd tasted beer only once or twice in his life.

"Well, I like beer a lot, 'specially on hot days like this."

Jim looked hard at Herbert's face. It was quiet, wondering, genuinely puzzled about people's reluctance to let him have beer.

"I'll get us some," the boy said.

"You think you should?" Herbert was actually whispering.

"Sure. They won't know."

He bided his time. When Uncle Peter's wagon was almost unloaded, the boy ran down the granary steps and shouted over the din, "Gotta go." This was an excuse that needed no explanation, and the men didn't even look up.

At the house, the boy darted around the corner and lifted the heavy trapdoor to the basement. From the table he took two freshly washed coffee mugs and tiptoed into the darkness. After some trial and error, he found how to make the spout work and filled the cups, spilling foam onto the floor and over his shoes. Once outside again, he had to set the brimming cups on the grass to close the door, bracing his feet so that he could close it without the usual thud. It wouldn't do to have his mother hear the door while the machines were still throbbing and the men still at work. He planned to hide in the long weeds along the fence until the men came up from the yard. Uncle Peter had already unhitched his team and would come with them. Herbert would be sent up to the granary to level the last bags of oats, and it would be safe to take the beer up then.

The boy squatted down into the grass and weeds. Sure enough, Carl throttled down the tractor and started up the hill toward the house. Louie, Philip, Uncle Peter, and Isador followed him. Just then they heard voices from the cow lane and Pa's wagon rounded the barn. Cy and Jake and the Tomchek boys were all riding on top of a half-load, the last load of the harvest, their pitchforks sticking up like spears against the sky. The boy felt his stomach beginning to hurt. They would start to unload, and Pa would ask where he was.

The men slid off the wagon, shouting to the yard crew while Pa reined in the horses next to the thresh machine. Cy and Jake raced up the hill. By the time Pa got down from the wagon, more than half the men in the yard were less than ten feet from Jim's hiding place. They talked and jostled each other for a minute and then looked for some signal from the boy's father, who had his hands on his hips and was squinting up at the sun. Finally, he shrugged.

"I guess we got time for a little drink before doin' this load," he said, breaking into a grin. Cy and Jake let out a whoop, and Philip made his wheezing noise. Pa started up toward them slowly, so that George and Jim Tomchek would understand that they were to follow him.

The boy could feel sweat collecting in his eyebrows and sliding from his throat onto his chest. His thigh muscles were burning from being cramped at such an acute angle, but he didn't dare to move. Maybe they would smell the beer. He knew you could smell beer even after someone had swallowed it. In his own nostrils, the smell was sharp, stinging. It seemed hours before all of the men had passed him and rounded the corner of the house. Jim sat down, muffling his groans as he stretched his legs in front of him, but even now he didn't get up. Sure enough, John appeared in the door of the mow and climbed down. Only after he had trotted around the house did the boy move up into a crouch and run along the fence to the granary. The beer, which had lost all its foam, sloshed out of the mugs and down into the weeds. By the time he got up the steps, each cup was only half-full.

Herbert was sitting on the rim of the grain bin, his knees up close to his shoulders.

"You got some?" He was still whispering.

"A little." The boy was whispering too; it was contagious. "Here, you can have it." He poured one cup into the other.

"No, you gotta have some."

"Just a little. I don't really like it that much." Jim thought he might never drink beer as long as he lived. Herbert poured about three tablespoons back into the empty cup, and the boy accepted it as he sank down next to him. Herbert drank the beer slowly, running his tongue around his lips after each drink. To Jim, the

few sips were hard to swallow, as bitter to his mouth as the smell
had been to his nose. When they were done, Jim buried the cups
in some grain at the far side of the room.

"Your ma won't miss 'em?" Herbert looked worried.

"Sure, but I'll get them later and say I found them somewhere else."

"You're real smart, Jimmy."

When the half-load was empty, lunch was already on the
table. Pa, Uncle Peter, and Jake carried the barrel outside and the
men had beer instead of coffee with their food. Sauerkraut, potato
dumplings, spareribs, and steaming sausage were handed around
in heavy bowls. The long table was noisier than usual as all
thirteen members of the crew joined in the loud celebration. Pa
had made a point of seeing to it that Herbert had some beer too,
now that the machines were silent.

"Ma used to grind it herself in a little mill," Herbert said
suddenly, very loudly. A silence fell, and everyone turned to look
at him in his place near the middle of the table.

"You know, Herbert," Philip said, "nobody ever knows what
the hell you're talking about."

Herbert looked first worried and then hurt. "Jim does,"
he said.

"No, I don't," the boy said hastily; he was two places away
from Herbert.

"Why, Jimmy," Philip said, "I was sure you talked the same
language as old Herbert here."

"I do not," the boy said, his face burning.

"You know what I heard?" Cy called from his end of the
table. "I heard that guys who get shortchanged upstairs get blessed
other places."

"Yeah," Jake laughed. "Come on, Herbert. Take down your
pants and show us what you got."

All of the men began to laugh and shout encouragement at
Herbert, all except the Tomchek boys, who turned their identical
faces out toward the field. They'd been in the army too, but unlike

Philip, who'd never been out of the country, they had actually fought in the war, George having to leave his wife and baby son behind. Whatever had happened to them in France, it had made them quiet.

"Come on, Herbert. Do it," the men were chanting.

The hurt look faded, and a foolish smile spread across Herbert's face. He pulled himself up from the table, setting nearby dishes shaking and clinking. Slowly, with winks in all directions, he began to undo his suspenders. The howling and laughter got louder, and he began to unbutton his pants.

". . . about enough now!" Pa's voice became audible above the noise. "That's enough. Come on, you guys. I got womenfolk going in and out here."

The laughs subsided into groans of disappointment.

"Sit down, Herbert," Pa said, but he was smiling in a friendly way.

The boy felt a powerful urge to punch Herbert, to just reach out and smack him on his silly grin.

After lunch, the boy's father said to him, "You and Herbert go down and close up the mow and the granary and take some hay to the horses. Put the tractor away too. Dan Stahl will bring his own tractor to get the threshing machine."

On the way down the hill, the boy half-ran to stay ahead of Herbert, but the big man soon caught up.

"What's the matter?" he said.

"Why do you do that?" the boy said between his teeth, not looking around.

"What?"

"Whatever they tell you to do? Why do you let them tease you?"

"Cuz they laugh then. We have a good time then."

The boy whirled to look at him. The innocent eyes were surrounded by worried wrinkles; the big hands were still holding the loose suspenders, snapping the ends open and closed.

"Aw, just forget it," the boy said and stalked down toward the barn.

When they'd finished all their jobs and returned to the house, the table was cleared, and the men were still working on the beer. It was almost one-thirty.

"I suppose we'd better get goin'," Peter said. "If we keep this up, the horses will have to find the way home for us."

The other men mumbled agreement, but no one seemed eager to leave. John had fallen asleep under the box elder tree. Philip and Carl had their heads together over the barrel.

"Where you goin' next, Herbert?" Pa asked.

"Up to Stahls'," Herbert answered, pointing to the west. At the top of a long hill and more than a mile away, the Stahls' barn roof was visible in the shimmering haze of heat. "I'll sleep there tonight."

"Why don't you take some beer along?" Philip said. They all looked at him. He was smiling widely, his face splotched all over with bright red patches. "How about it, Matt?" Philip addressed the boy's father.

"Sure, sure. Herbert can have some beer. Get a water pail, Jimmy."

"No, no," Philip said. "Why doesn't he just take the barrel?" There was a confused silence. Philip rocked the barrel, and it made a sloshing sound.

"Must be almost a gallon of beer left in there," Philip said. "Tell you what, Herbert. If you can carry this barrel all the way to Stahls' barn, you can have all the beer that's left. We all had enough, right fellas?"

"Sure, sure," the other men murmured.

"That be all right, Matt?" Philip said. "You could pick up the barrel tomorrow on your way into town."

"I suppose," Pa said, still looking a little puzzled.

"Now here's the deal, Herbert," Philip said, coming forward. "You gotta carry the barrel to that barn, without once setting it down on the ground, and you can't get down with your knees on the ground to rest. If you can do that, you get the beer. We'll go along to see you don't cheat."

Herbert looked at Pa, who nodded, a smile starting at the corners of his mouth. The big man raised his arms above his head once, twice; his joy could find no words. Cy and Jake came forward, sensing a good finish to the harvest, after all. They had been drinking fast to catch up with the yard crew.

"We gotta go home, boys," Peter said.

"Come on, Pa," Jake protested. "John has to sleep it off some more anyway."

"Oh, all right," Peter said. "We can go along to Stahls' for a bit."

The men formed a circle around Herbert and the barrel. Only the boy and the Tomchek brothers still sat at the table. George Tomchek had a look on his face as if he'd tasted something he didn't like.

"I'm gonna hitch up the team, Pa," he said. "We got chores at home need doin'."

Old Isador stopped chewing for a moment and looked hard at his two sons. Then he spat disgustedly.

"All right. Guess you're right. We'll be seein' you next week, Matt."

"Sure, Isador," Pa said and then turned back into the circle. Even he looked like he was beginning to feel the effects of the beer.

"Now you get a good grip on it, Herbert," Louie said, as Herbert squatted to wrap his arms around the barrel. It was an eight-gallon container, a quarter-barrel, three feet high and fat, made of heavy wood to keep its contents cool for as long as possible. The iron bands added to its weight.

Herbert stood up, holding the barrel against his chest and stomach, his face flashing a buck-toothed smile, his nostrils flaring with excitement. As the Tomcheks made their way toward their wagon, Herbert started off toward the road, the circle of men spreading out on both sides of him. The boy watched the

Tomcheks for a moment and then stood up to follow his father, who was in the back ranks of the escort heading for Stahls' barn.

Before Herbert had gone many yards up the road, it must have occurred to him that he'd chosen the wrong method of carrying the barrel. His long arms could barely close around it, and the muscle strain was already beginning to show; his forearms began to tremble. Suddenly, he squatted down in the middle of the road, resting the barrel on his knees. He teetered slightly and then regained his balance.

"Watch it, Herbert," Cy shouted. "You can't sit down."

Herbert had stopped smiling, but only because he was concentrating. Carefully, he maneuvered the barrel up onto his left shoulder, holding it front and back with his big hands. Then he stood up suddenly and strode forward, breaking into a grin again. The going was better now and they made good progress up the hill, the men shouting encouragement to the burdened man. The boy trailed behind. It was very hot.

Halfway up the hill, Herbert slowed down. Sweat was pouring off his face, some of it getting into his eyes. He stopped for a moment, freed his right hand, and wiped his eyes. The barrel pitched forward dangerously, wood and iron digging into his shoulder. The circle of men gasped as Herbert's hand shot up to steady the barrel. The big man rocked, then steadied. His maimed right foot groped ahead of him.

"Gettin' tired, are you, Herbert?" Philip crowed, mopping his own red face with a large handkerchief.

"Come on, Herbert! You can do it," Carl shouted, bringing his face up close to Herbert's so that his nose was almost touching the straining jaw.

Herbert turned halfway around and caught sight of Jim. They looked steadily at each other for a few seconds, and then Herbert smiled.

"I'm fine," he said. "Here we go."

His characteristic way of walking, with that forward lean, was exaggerated now, and he moved slowly. Cy and Jake danced all the way around him every five steps or so, chanting, "Come on Herbert. Come on Herbert." At about three-quarters of a mile, the big man stopped again and began to sag forward.

"Here he goes, here he goes," Philip crowed. "Get ready to yell, 'Timber.'"

"He's gonna be all right, aren't you, Herbert?" Pa said, laughing a little.

Herbert went into a squat again and very slowly slid the barrel onto his knees. From behind, the boy noticed a red stain on the flannel shirt; his shoulder was bleeding. The boy lifted his hand and stretched it toward the crouching figure, but he was too far behind to reach him. Then, quickly, he put his hand inside his pocket, glancing up to see if the others had noticed his gesture.

"What ya gonna do now, Herbert?" Philip sneered.

Herbert lifted his face to look up at them. His straw-colored hair was plastered in wet, spiky clumps to his forehead, and streams of sweat made dirty, brownish trails in the dust on his face. The boy had come up even with him by this time, and he thought that the pale, starting eyes looked almost blind. Herbert raised his hand and passed it down over his face once from eyebrows to throat before grabbing the barrel to steady it once more. His eyes focused on the boy, and his mouth moved slightly, but he didn't speak. Instead, he began to slide the barrel up toward his right shoulder, his head leaning forward so far that it was almost between his knees. Carl and Philip danced backwards so that the faltering head would not touch their trouser legs. One of the iron bands caught on Herbert's collar bone, and he made a gasping sound. He managed to shrug the barrel up onto his right shoulder but almost fell backward as he did so.

"Remember, you can't sit down," Carl shouted. Cy and Jake had fallen silent.

Then slowly, incredibly, Herbert stood up, staggering backward and then forward again, leaning into the hill at a seemingly impossible angle. Stahls' barn was very near now, only its tin roof shimmering in the heat. The boy found that he was walking next to Herbert, at his right side, so close that the barrel was suspended above his head. His legs felt heavy, as if something was dragging at them from below. The progress was very slow and the other men had come to a stop a little ahead of Herbert.

"Not so far to go now," Philip called. "Hurry up!"

Herbert had stopped. He lifted his right foot, but then set it down again in the same place. Slowly, he went into his squat, sliding the barrel onto his knees. A thin red stain in the dirty flannel followed the barrel as it slid, spreading out slowly into scalloped edges.

Herbert raised his face to look at the boy. Veins were standing out in his temples, and the boy could see them throbbing. The misshapen mouth formed a word without sound. The boy's hands were jammed deep inside his overall pockets. He looked up at the group of men, looked at his father. Pa's face was knotted in a frown, but he made no sign.

Before the boy could look down again, Herbert had rolled forward onto his knees. The barrel hit the road with a hollow thud. Herbert let out one long howl and threw his upper body onto the barrel. The other men ran forward to circle him. When he lifted his face again, tears were streaming into the tracks already made by the sweat. The now-dimmed eyes found the boy and held him; no one else among the faces bending over him seemed to interest the fallen man.

The boy began to back away. He couldn't stop the tears that stung his eyes, and he couldn't turn his face to hide them. He stumbled and fell hard, shredding the skin of his palms against the gravel as he tried to break his fall. Immediately, he scrambled up and, this time, was able to wrench himself around to run forward down the hill. Within a few yards, his father had caught him and spun him around again. The boy struggled to escape, would not look up.

"Hold on." His father's voice was quiet, intense. "What's the matter with you?"

The boy pulled hard against the man's grip, the muscles of his upper arms aching under the powerful hands which held them. His father gave him one quick shake, rolling the boy's head backwards so that the tear-blinded face looked up at him.

"Be a man." Pa spoke through his teeth so that the near-whisper had a whistling sound.

The boy squinted hard so that he could focus on his father's face. The familiar gray eyes widened slightly, the grip loosened a little.

"We're going to give him the beer. We always meant to give him the beer. Don't you know that? It was a joke. It doesn't make any difference."

Jim found his voice, at first choked and then steadily louder.

"It does make a difference. It does! It makes a difference!"

His father let go of him very suddenly, and he started down the hill again, backwards, shouting again and again the conviction he could not have explained if his father had asked him how or why, screaming it at the men who turned from the kneeling figure at the top of the hill to stare open-mouthed, uncomprehending, at his retreat.

Burying Pal

(1959)

The huge body lay half on its side, half on its back, the front legs sticking stiffly up into the air. The back legs, where the chains were attached, were pulled backward at a sharp angle, giving the dead horse the appearance of springing sideways across the surface of the field. The tractor, which had dragged the corpse down the cow lane to this pasture at the edge of the woods, was still hooked to the body by the chains that seemed to hold the animal back.

Jacob Himrich stood at the edge of a deep pit he'd dug the day before with a borrowed backhoe. He was trying to figure out how to get the horse into the pit without tipping his small tractor. If he'd still had the backhoe, he could have attached it to the chains and driven it straight through, pulling the horse behind, but Dave Drossart had needed his machine back almost immediately.

"Well, Pal," Jake said, addressing the grayish brown body, "I suppose I'll have to get you to the edge and just let you roll down." Talking to Pal was an old habit for Jake, and he didn't see any reason to stop just because the horse was dead.

Jake was so used to driving the John Deere that he had little trouble maneuvering it along the edge of the hole. In low gear, the tractor moved slowly enough to bring the horse's body to the point where it was literally teetering on the edge. Then Jake climbed down, carefully removed the chains from Pal's legs, and started the horse's slide by heaving against the rigid front legs. He watched the body slide, glad that the legs didn't catch anywhere on the way down. Pal's body was already bloated so that he slid like a barrel; he'd been dead two days, and it was a particularly hot and muggy July this year. The horse came to rest almost in the center of the pit, and Jake looked down at it for a long moment before carrying a shovel toward the heap of dirt that lined the north edge of the hole.

Winter Roads, Summer Fields

Dave Drossart had been more than a little surprised that Jake wanted to bury his horse.

"Why don't you just call Kinnard's?" he'd asked. "They'll come out with a truck and haul him away."

"No," Jake had answered. "I want to do it this way."

"Well, I wish I could give you more help, but I got this foundation to dig for the Fredericks' new machine shed."

"That's okay. I'll finish the job myself once the hole is dug."

"You're nuts, Jake. You could kill yourself in this weather trying to move that much dirt back by hand."

"I'll take it slow. Don't worry about it."

Jake didn't often tell people what he was feeling, so he couldn't even try to make Dave understand why he wouldn't send Pal to Kinnard's. It wasn't just that Pal had been with him since he took the farm over from his father. It was that Jake had worked at Kinnard's for over five months the year before. Dave would never understand what that had been like.

Harley Kinnard, who'd gone to school with Jake, had been a nervous, discontented kid who took his first chance to get out of farming. By the time he was twenty-five, he had a small mink ranch near Green Bay, and by the time he was thirty-five, he was very nearly a rich man. He'd built his own processing plant to produce mink food, a slaughterhouse where discarded horses were butchered and ground up to feed Harley's cash crop.

When Jake had asked Harley for a part-time job last year, their childhood friendship had made his acceptance almost automatic. Besides, Jake was a good butcher, skilled with a knife, and strong. For almost twenty years, he'd done butchering for his neighbors as well as for his own family's needs. Jake felt no compunction about killing cows and pigs, but he hated to kill horses. Cows and pigs were a living, but horses and dogs were workmates, companions, almost people.

At Harley's slaughterhouse, horses were often brought in after they'd already died, old horses that had just tipped over in a field or a stall. It didn't bother Jake to "process" these animals, but he never got over feeling queasy about the other ones, the ones brought in still walking. He had to lead them into a chute, hold a rifle at a downward angle against their foreheads, and then pull the trigger. The horses almost always came into the chute easily, trustingly, used to going wherever a man would lead them. Then Jake would bleed the downed animal into a long, sloping gutter and open the belly to remove the intestines. Next he made expert cuts around the head and ankles, attached chains to the hide on the back legs, and started the engine which would strip off the hide all in one piece. Both blood and hide were sold to other contractors. With a powerful meat saw, Jake first quartered the carcass and then cut each piece in half again. He could then carry the pieces to the grinder, a fierce, noisy machine that ground up the horse, bones and all, after Jake had dropped the pieces through a safety door.

As he began to scoop loose dirt down onto Pal's body, Jake was remembering how much he'd hated that job at Kinnard's. It was the only extended job he'd ever had away from the farm, and he wouldn't have taken it if the economy hadn't been so bad in the fifties that his savings had been wiped out. It made Jake nervous to go into debt, so in February of '58 he'd asked Harley for the job. He had to pay for the funeral, and for the headstone—for Jimmy's headstone.

Even now, more than a year later, Jake had to steel himself to let Jimmy's death into his mind. To die of measles! A kid's disease that everybody went through. The other three kids had it first, all of them feverish and whiny at the same time, right over Christmas. It was already the new year when Jimmy complained one morning of a sore throat and feeling hot. Jake's wife, Anna, had put Jimmy in their big bed downstairs, right next to the kitchen. In the early afternoon, she sent little Paul to find Jake, to tell him that Jimmy was "acting funny."

Jake shoveled harder, remembering; sweat poured down his face and throat, but he wasn't really seeing the dirt falling onto Pal's bloated side. He saw again the bed as it had looked when he came through the door that winter afternoon—the whole bed shaking from the force of Jimmy's convulsions. When Jimmy stopped twitching, Jake had pulled him up onto his chest, feeling the shock of the high fever through his own cold clothes. Jimmy had stopped breathing. Jake squeezed his body, blew into his mouth, finally even pounded on the little chest, but nothing worked. Anna had screamed and wept, clung to the other children, who wailed in their high, thin voices. But Jake had stayed on the bed, stone-faced, holding Jimmy's body until it began to feel cool, the fever leaving at last, now that it had killed him. He had been seven years old.

The funeral offended Jake. To see his son lying against white satin inside a metal box made him feel not sad but angry. Embalmed, bloodless, the face had to be colored with makeup to make it look human, but Jake could see the makeup, could smell the hair oil which made Jimmy's blond hair look unnaturally dark. Jake spent two days listening numbly to the murmured words of family and friends, when all he wanted to do was to get a washrag and scrub Jimmy's face clean again.

The cemetery had been the worst part of the whole business. Watching the coffin lowered into the newly poured vault, Jake had to hold in his impulse to snatch it back. He'd wanted to shout, "Let me take him home!" If they could put him in Himrich ground, have him there as they went about the business of planting and harvesting, watching the seasons turn, it wouldn't seem so bad. Leaving him among strangers in this field that was not theirs seemed cruel, like a betrayal. But Jake didn't speak or move. And he didn't cry either. That came only later, when some of the anger was gone.

By this time, Jake's shirt was soaked with sweat, and he was breathing hard. Pal's back legs and hindquarters were almost covered with dirt. Jake squinted up at the setting sun and decided to rest for a while. Anna and Henry were doing the milking, so he didn't have to go back until this job was done. Henry was twelve now, a big help on the farm and a good boy too. He'd taken Jimmy's death hard because Paul, the baby of the family, was not a good substitute playmate—too young, too much his mother's pet. The girl, Frances, was nine now, just finished with the third grade, a smart child who the nuns said had "great potential." Jake loved all his children, was proud of them, but Jimmy had been special to him. Bow-legged and clumsy—a "regular little duppus," Jake had called him—he'd also been a cheerful, sunny little boy, seemingly unaware of danger, careening through life with ragged clothes and dirty feet.

Looking down at Pal's body, Jake found himself remembering the times he'd given the kids rides, on hayracks in the summer and sleds in the winter, with the team of horses making their harnesses ring. Pal had been there from the first, since before the kids, and there had been three teammates, the last one a chestnut mare named Fanny. When Jake bought the John Deere in 1957, he'd sold Fanny to George Frederick, but he couldn't bring himself to sell Pal. There had never been a better horse, no harder worker, no gentler partner. Even in Pal's old age, he had allowed the kids to ride around on his back in the pasture, coming when they called him, stopping when they yelled "Whoa!" And he even put up with the series of horses Jake had brought home from Kinnard's.

Jake had to smile to himself, remembering those horses. He ran them over in his mind as he got back up and began shoveling again. It was almost seven-thirty now, but the heat of the day hadn't lessened very much. The air felt heavy against his body as he scooped the damp earth into the hole. Oh yes, Pal had been a saint about those other horses.

Not all of the animals sold to Kinnard's were old. Some of them looked relatively young and strong and, because Harley never bought sick horses, Jake knew they were healthy too. He puzzled over why farmers would sell such animals to Harley for slaughter. It made sense to sell a horse you couldn't use anymore, but a young horse could always be sold to some other farmer who needed it. There didn't seem to be any good reason to kill these horses and feed them to mink.

The second month Jake was working at Kinnard's, a young farmer brought in a big, roan-colored gelding, no more than four years old. Harley paid twenty dollars for the horse and put it into the corral with the old horses waiting to die.

"Why do you suppose he wants to sell a fine-looking animal like that?" Jake asked.

"Beats me," Harley said. "I never ask that. As long as the animal's healthy and the guy'll take my offer, that's all I need to know."

"It's a shame," Jake said. "Look how quiet and well behaved he is."

"It's nothing to me," Harley said.

"Maybe I could use him at home," Jake said, after a pause.

Harley eyed him narrowly for a moment.

"You mean buy him back from me?" he asked.

"Sure," Jake shrugged. "Young horse like that, must have lots of good years left in him yet."

"Okay," Harley said. "But there must be some reason that guy wanted to bring the horse here. You give it a try, and if it works out, you just pay me the twenty bucks. If not, bring him back."

Jake took the red gelding home that day and stalled him next to Pal in the barn. On Saturday, he got out the old harnesses to hitch the team to the manure spreader. The new horse stood calmly next to Pal while Jake worked the straps and buckles. Pal seemed a little excited about getting back to work, but he was as well behaved as always. Jake climbed up onto the seat, took up the reins, and said gently, "Giddup." Pal started forward at once, lifting his big hooves in his old rhythm, but the roan didn't move at all. The harnesses heaved sideways, the whippletree creaked, and Pal came to a stop.

"Giddup," Jake shouted, slapping the reins, and Pal started forward again, dragging the whippletree even more askew as the roan leaned back into the harness, bracing his legs stiffly out in front of him.

"Whoa," Jake called and climbed down from the manure spreader. He went around to the horses' heads and gently backed Pal up a few paces until the team was almost even again. Then he grabbed the roan's halter in both hands and said, "Giddup." Pal walked ahead and Jake pulled with all his strength on the halter. The roan leaned back, his front hooves sliding on the frozen ground. Between them, Jake and Pal managed to drag the other horse a few feet forward, even though the whippletree had turned sideways enough to dig into the stubborn animal's side. Then the red horse simply sat down, and the weight of its rump was enough to permit the stiff front legs to hold their ground. Pal stopped, turned his head far enough to see past his blinders, and just looked at Jake.

On Monday, Jake took the roan back to Kinnard's.

"Balky," he said in answer to Harley's questioning look.

"Poor old Pal," Jake said, leaning on the shovel and looking down at the horse's head, the only part of the body not yet dirtied by the ground. The belly still rose up above the dark earth, but the lower body was already covered. Jake sat down, pulled out his pocket handkerchief, and mopped his face. His hair felt as wet as if he'd washed it. Dave Drossart was right about this being a crazy thing to do; it would take hours to finish the job, and the temperature probably wouldn't go much below eighty degrees the whole time.

Jake looked down the cow lane toward the buildings. He could see the lights in the house and the silhouette of the barn against the gray of the evening sky. The woods behind him formed one edge of the small farm, and the buildings were at the other edge. In between was rich, dark land like the mounds around him, good growing land for hay and oats and corn, land that smelled wonderful when Jake turned it over with the plow every fall, smelled good to him even now when he was hot and tired. His shoulders ached, and the insteps of his feet throbbed. He was forty years old now, still powerful and fit, but not as resilient as he'd been even five years ago. Halfway, he often thought, remembering that his father had died at eighty; halfway.

After about twenty minutes of rest, Jake began shoveling again, this time on the edge near Pal's head, throwing the earth quickly and not looking down at the gray-spotted muzzle below him. Only when the head was covered did he turn on the tractor lights to see what he was doing.

Jake had brought the second horse home from Kinnard's in April, just three months after Jimmy's funeral. It was a handsome animal, almost palomino in color, bigger than Pal, and only about eight years old. Jake hitched the team to a hay wagon loaded with posts he needed to replace an old wooden fence that separated the Himrich farm from the Tomchek farm on the northeast.

The horses moved well together, not fast because Pal no longer moved fast, but steadily and smoothly. Why on earth, Jake wondered, did that farmer think this horse should be sold for slaughter? At the first gate, Jake called "Whoa," and the horses came immediately to a stop, waiting quietly as Jake climbed down and walked in front of them to open the fence. He'd just put the wires onto the ground, off to the right of the gate, when he heard a crashing sound behind him: a great noise of harnesses and then a thud. He turned to see the palomino-colored horse on its side on the ground, its head lolling over and then coming to rest against the hard-packed earth of the cow lane.

Jake ran over to the team and steadied Pal, who was prancing a little in alarm, his eyes rolling in an effort to see what had happened next to him, his mouth working the bit. For a moment, Jake thought the horse had simply dropped dead. He bent over its head and placed his hand on its neck. The animal's chest was rising and falling in a familiar rhythm; he was asleep. Jake pounded and kicked the horse, cursing under his breath, until it got back up onto its feet. Before the short trip to the end of the farm could be completed, the horse had fallen over twice more. Jake could see it going to sleep whenever they stopped; allowing it to stand for more than a minute was, he learned, unwise. He just let the horse lie there while he unloaded the posts, and then, after slugging it awake again, forced the horses into a lumbering trot all the way home. Pal was badly winded and soaking wet by the time they got to the barnyard. The sleeper went back to Kinnard's the next day.

Why hadn't he just given it up, Jake wondered now as he shoveled on into the growing dark. Surely twice was enough to teach him a lesson. But every time he saw a horse at Kinnard's that looked good, that seemed too young for the grinder, he began to think he might try it again. Getting foolish in his old age probably, he told himself now, instead of wiser. Pal's body was no longer visible, and the pit was nearly full. Jake climbed up onto the tractor, started it up, and carefully maneuvered the big wheels back and forth over the ground he'd been shoveling. The tractor bounced and sank down into the loose earth, but the lowest gear always pulled it out again. The ground packed down under the wheels, and soon the pit's surface was crisscrossed with tire tracks. Jake climbed down again and went back to shoveling, his half hour on the tractor enough to make him feel rested.

The third horse had been a mare, a big, clumsy-looking animal that her owner said was "too dumb to teach anything." She was young, though, and seemed very tame, nuzzling up to Jake when he took her halter. In some ways she reminded him of Fanny.

"Kids spoiled her rotten," the farmer had said, "and after that I couldn't do a thing with her. If I tried to sell her to somebody for a workhorse, he'd come back and bust my chops for cheating him with this worthless nag."

"I'd like to give her a try," Jake had told Harley.

"You're a stubborn man, Jake Himrich," Harley had said.

"No, it's just that it's busy on the farm at this time of year.

The boy drives the tractor now, and I can use a team. She probably just needs patience, and my other horse has lots of that."

The first time he tried to hitch up the horses, Jake put Pal into the harness first and then brought out the mare. She followed him easily and then stood still as long as he held her halter, but just as soon as Jake let go to pick up the harness, she just walked away. She didn't seem to be in any hurry, just walking slowly, but she wouldn't stop when Jake yelled "Whoa!" Again and again, Jake tried to get the mare into harness, but every time he found it necessary to let go of her halter, she would simply wander off. Finally, Jake called Henry to help him by holding the mare's halter while he slapped the harness onto her.

But it was no better once she was hooked up. She didn't seem to understand about stopping; she just kept walking when Jake told the team to whoa. Pal became badly confused, coming to a dutiful stand when told to and then starting out again as the big mare dragged him forward. After a half-hour of this, Jake gave up and separated the two horses, tying the mare to the barn door. But he kept her in harness after he'd turned Pal out into the pasture. Then he and Henry took her around to the back of the barn where the land roller was still parked, its heavy cylinder slightly sunk into the wet ground.

Jake attached the harness to the metal frame on the side edge of the land roller, hoping to anchor the mare to something she couldn't move. Then he told Henry to let go of her head. As usual, she began walking away at once, coming to the end of her harness straps very quickly. She stopped only briefly, then leaned forward into the harnesses, digging her hooves down into the mud.

"Whoa," Jake shouted. "Whoa, you knothead."

The mare strained even harder, her rear flanks buckling a little as she pulled. The land roller lurched a bit and then began to slide. The mare straightened and began, slowly, to walk away, the roller gaining momentum as it overcame its rut.

"What should we do?" Henry asked. "Should we grab her head?"

Burying Pal

"No," Jake said. "Let her wear herself out dragging a land roller sideways. Let her take it all the way to Hammern, if she wants to. That'll teach her to stop when I tell her to."

Jake walked beside the straining horse, occasionally saying "whoa" directly into her flattened ear, but she just kept plodding along. By the time they were halfway across the field, the mare was wheezing like an asthmatic and her sides were heaving. At last she stopped.

"Good," Jake shouted. "This is what 'whoa' means, you blockheaded idiot." He looked back toward the barn, sighing over the trench the land roller had made in the pasture.

The mare stood for a few minutes, gasping. Then she leaned into the harness and started the land roller down the other side of the sloping field toward the creek. Jake kept at her side, walking slowly and yelling at regular intervals for her to stop, but she only paused for breath before lumbering on. After almost an hour of this scarring up of a perfectly good pasture, Jake gave up.

The day he took the mare back to Kinnard's was a slow day. In the afternoon, Jake went across the road with Harley to watch the mink eat. It was the first time Jake had been there, and he was almost overwhelmed by the smell. In his life as a farmer, he believed that he'd got used to any animal smell, but compared to this evil stench, even pigs were fragrant, healthy, clean. If Harley hadn't been with him, Jake would have pulled out his handkerchief and held it over his face. The mink looked like smaller versions of the weasel he'd once caught in his chicken coop—long, sleek bodies and little, ratlike heads. Harley made him walk through almost all the rows of tiered cages, looking on while hundreds and hundreds of mink gulped their meat, fresh from the grinder, still bright bluish red. At the end of the day, Jake quit his job at Kinnard's.

"Busy time of year at home," he mumbled to Harley.

"You caught up on those payments?" Harley asked.

"Sure. All caught up."

Winter Roads, Summer Fields

Now, more than a year later, it was as if Jake could still smell the mink just by thinking about them. He'd heaped the last loose ground into a little hill over the pit where Pal was buried. It was pitch dark by now, still hot and humid, and he could see only by the headlights of the tractor. The first time he'd used the tractor to tamp the ground, he'd had to drive down into the pit; now he drove the John Deere up over the mound, again and again, packing the ground until the mound rose only a little above the surface of the field. Then he turned the tractor and brought it to a stop, motor still throbbing, so that the headlights shone over his finished work. In a few weeks, he would seed the place again with clover and alfalfa.

He knew the mound would rise a little at first as the body bloated larger and began to rot. But eventually it would go down again. The dark earth would sink through Pal's body, taking his meat back into itself; it would fill up his big rib cage and get inside his bony head. Then the surface would go back to normal, just as if no one had ever dug it up. Jake wondered how many years this circle would be a brighter green than the rest of the field. Well, he would find out, he thought, putting the tractor into gear again; he would be right here to see it, spring and fall, hot and cold. He and Pal were not going anywhere.

Pin Money

(1964)

Joanne looked down the cow's flank, watching for any movement
of the hind legs. Her reddened hands worked away automatically,
stripping milk into a battered aluminum pail. In the next
stanchion, she could hear her husband removing the milking
machine from another cow; it was there she would go next to
collect milk the machine had left behind, milk to feed the cats and
for their own use in the house. She'd lived on the farm for six years
and had become efficient at these chores, but she'd never learned to
feel comfortable around the cows. Every time one of them stamped
a foot or shifted its weight, she was seized by a spasm of fear. The
inevitable swishing of manure-stained tails over her head as she
milked filled her with disgust. To her it seemed that the huge
brutes were malevolent, were deliberately feigning stupidity in
order to trick her into an error that would leave her vulnerable to
some turning of their slumberous power against her.

She stood up now, lifted the half-filled bucket in one hand and
the stool in the other, and stepped out across the gutter. She was a
tall, rawboned woman with a forward-thrusting head, thin hair,
and pale, lashless eyes behind wire-rimmed glasses. Seen from a
distance, she might have been any age. Only her smooth cheeks
showed how young she was.

"Are you going out to seed corn today?" she said to her
husband's back.

Frank turned slowly, raising his head from its habitual angle
to focus on her. He always looked a bit dreamy when he did this,
as if he'd just been wakened from sleep.

"Mmm," he said before turning away again. But this brief
response was enough to remind Joanne of how handsome he was.
Even in his barn clothes, she thought, he looked elegant, tall and
trim. His hair curled out from under the baseball cap which

shaded his eyes—large, pale brown eyes with yellow flecks all around the edges of the irises. His soft, almost feminine mouth was clouded by a thick mustache that showed traces of gray at the outer edges.

She'd never got over her own surprise at having married such a good-looking man. When he had first asked her out, she'd suspected a mistake, believed that he'd confused her name with some other girl he'd seen in church. After their first date, her mother had said appreciatively, "I wonder how he managed to escape for so long," for he was already over thirty.

So it hadn't mattered to Joanne that he was poor, that they had to go to the movies in his pickup truck, that her coworkers at the store had laughed at him and called him "farmer boy." She hadn't even minded that he almost never spoke. She'd gone through high school without a date, one of those girls no one ever seemed to notice, so she had only a hazy idea of how courtship was supposed to go. Frank Volkman was hardworking and respected at church for taking care of his blind mother. When he proposed, she agreed at once to marry him, leaving the job she'd held for only a year after high school to move to the small dairy farm where he had been born. And she'd learned to drive a tractor, pitch bales of hay, milk cows. But they never got a Grade A rating for their dairy, never seemed to make much headway against the filth and the flies, never found the milk checks big enough to do much more than cover expenses.

After they finished the milking, Frank left for the house without a word or a look. Joanne detoured to a small door at the side of the barn; she had to stoop to get inside a boarded-up stall where she stood for a moment surveying the floor. Small puffs of life moved back and forth under the bright light of two heating lamps which Joanne had hung from an overhead socket. The faint cheeping which she'd heard from outside the door got louder as she moved forward among the chicks to look into the shallow pans of ground feed and the circular water trough, both of which she'd filled that morning before the milking. She knew there would still be plenty of food and water, but she liked to check several times a day, liked just to be in the room. There were forty-nine chicks in all, little balls of yellow fluff; there had been fifty when they arrived the week before. The one she lost had looked bad from the first, scrawny, its reddened eyes bulging out of its head, its neck almost without feathers. Still, she had grieved when it died, worried over the others though they looked all right.

She looked around the little chicken coop with satisfaction. The walls were covered from the floor to about her waist with gritty brown tar paper patterned in the shapes of bricks. Ten years ago, before her marriage to him, Frank had re-sided the house with this paper. She'd found a half-roll of the siding in the granary and had taken it without asking to make this room snug, for the walls were rough planks with large cracks and holes between them. The siding had run out before she could finish, but, she reasoned, the chicks were too small to get above the papered area, and spring had cooperated with the heating lamps to keep the floor warm enough for the babies. Joanne smiled as she looked all around the room once again before stepping back outside.

Weariness seemed to settle on her once again as she moved up toward the house, a low frame structure with sagging porches and battered, rusting eaves. The brown siding was faded and tattered, hardly recognizable as the same covering that looked so new and cheerful in the chicken coop.

In the large room that was both kitchen and dining room, Joanne found her husband sitting next to the old wooden high chair that now held their son, a blond two-year-old wearing a dish towel for a bib. At the sink stood a tiny woman in a cotton print apron which almost eclipsed her dark dress; her white hair was pulled straight back from her face and twisted into a neat roll at the base of her neck. She turned her whole upper body toward the back door as Joanne came into the room. Her sightless eyes, so long covered by cataracts that only a few people could remember what color they had once been, had a milky, dead look.

"Is that you, Joanne?" she said in the harsh tone of voice that had become her habit, almost as if she thought her own blindness had made other people hard of hearing.

"Of course it's me, Ma," the young woman said without looking at her.

"Well, you're making me wait breakfast," the old woman said, querulous, perpetually offended. "Melissa! Melissa, baby, you can come for breakfast now."

A little girl ran into the room. Her flannel nightgown was faded and too short for her, her hair matted from sleep, but she was a beautiful child with honey-colored hair and a delicate face.

"What are we having, Gamma?" she asked in her bright, piping voice.

"Fried eggs and toast," the grandmother said, feeling her way to an old gas stove where a cast-iron pan was heating over a burner.

"I want French toast and jam," the little girl said.

"You eat what the rest of us eat, Melissa," Joanne said. "This is not a restaurant."

The child pursed her mouth, walked up to the old woman, and hugged her right leg.

"I can have French toast, can't I, Gamma?" she whispered.

"I'll see what I can find," the old woman said, putting her hands down onto the child's head and shoulders and lifting her face in the direction from which Joanne's voice had come.

Joanne looked sharply at Frank, who was swinging his pocket watch in front of the baby's face. He didn't look up, hadn't heard. He never lost his temper, never raised his voice, never interfered. In the beginning, Joanne had sometimes turned angrily on the old woman, but her husband had looked reproachful and had become even more silent. So now she was silent too.

As she looked around the room, from her husband and son to her daughter and mother-in-law, she thought bitterly of the many times other people, her own mother included, had told her how lucky she was to have "help with the kids." People thought the old woman was wonderful, so spry for seventy, so capable for a blind

Winter Roads, Summer Fields

person. Why, she even cooked! Joanne never had anything to say to those remarks, but she would have liked to show this scene to her mother, the old woman grasping the child, her blind face daring Joanne to defy her, while Frank seemed to enclose himself and the boy in a tight circle that no female was allowed to enter.

Yet the sight of Melissa always filled Joanne with aching love. It seemed to her miraculous that such a child could have come out of her body. Only Melissa was excepted from the resentment Joanne felt for beautiful females. It had always seemed to her so unfair that they should reap confidence, attention, love from something they'd never worked for, never earned. But Melissa was like a flower, blooming unselfconsciously to give joy. It hurt Joanne almost physically when the bright little head disappeared into the bedroom off the kitchen in answer to a harsh call, for she'd once heard the old woman saying, "Go see what your mama is doing and come tell me."

In the afternoons, the old woman turned on the tiny black-and-white television that sat on the corner of the table, and Melissa would keep up a running commentary—"Now they're kissing. Now he's opening the door"—all in her singsong, four-year-old's voice. Joanne felt it was just another of the old woman's methods for stealing the child—a deliberate, calculated kidnapping. But Joanne was powerless. She had no ally in the house.

And there was never any money. When she wanted to buy clothes for the kids or take Melissa to a Disney movie, there was no money. A doll Melissa had seen on television and begged for was impossible, even at Christmas. Slowly, over the past two years, Joanne had come to believe that everything in her life would be all right if only she had a little money of her own, if only she didn't have to ask Frank for every penny.

So she'd cut corners, scrimped, done without for almost a year, secretly hoarding up dimes and quarters, counting them in the evenings when Frank fell asleep at 8:30. She didn't stint on things for the children, but she hadn't bought new shoes for herself the whole year, got nothing for the house that wasn't absolutely necessary. She didn't care about the house anyway. During the first year of her marriage, she'd cleaned the cupboards and lined the shelves with bright paper. When the blind woman had reached for a glass, she'd lost control of it as it slid along the slippery new surface. Its crash had brought Joanne running up from the basement to find the old woman clinging to the sink, white with fury, crying out at the sound of Joanne's footsteps, "This is my house! My house!"

So all this hard winter Joanne had saved and, by early spring, she had enough for the chicks. She could see years into the future. The fifty hens would become a hundred, and then two hundred. The egg money would be enough to cover the costs of keeping them, with enough left over so that Melissa could have new nightgowns as soon as she outgrew the old ones, could maybe take ballet lessons in Green Bay, and the baby could have one of those riding toys that looked like a ladybug.

Only when she'd saved all the money did she tell Frank about her plan. They'd been feeding the cows, he forking hay while she followed behind with a pail of ground oats, scooping the fine mixture over the hay. When she finished her carefully rehearsed speech, he'd turned to her with that vague look in his yellow-flecked eyes.

"I don't like chickens," he said tonelessly.

"You won't have to go near them, Frank. I'll tend them all by myself."

"I mean, I don't know if I want them on the place. I'd almost rather have pigs."

"Pigs would be more work for you, though," she said quickly, thinking that, of course, pigs would be *his*, and therefore he would get to say what would be done with them. "And you already have too much to do, with the crops coming and all."

"Well, I don't know," he said after a long pause while staring in her direction with his eyes wide and dreamy. Sometimes when he looked like that, she thought he didn't see her at all; other times she suspected that it was just his way of resisting her, thwarting her, putting his will against her for some reason she couldn't understand.

"We could use the extra money," she said at last.

"Well, I suppose," he answered, "but you'll have to get some place ready for them, build some roosts. And only fifty. I don't really like chickens."

So she had taken her interim victory, rigged her makeshift brooder house, and bought the chicks. And because she'd won this much, she could swallow her anger now, quietly wash up for breakfast, and watch the old woman hunting for some jam to put on Melissa's French toast. When she had some money of her own, Joanne thought, she wouldn't have to let someone else decide what her children would have for breakfast.

After the meal, Frank took the tractor and the corn planter out to the farthest edge of the farm. Joanne washed the dishes and carefully cleaned the top of the stove, which was splattered with grease and spilled eggs. The blind woman seldom burned herself when she cooked, but she left chunks and spills of food all over the stove and countertop. When Melissa was dressed, Joanne gathered laundry and went down the perilously steep basement steps to do battle with the ancient, wringer washing machine. By late morning, towels and sheets were flapping on the line, and Joanne's fingers were red from bleach and hot water.

She put the baby down for his nap, standing next to him for a few minutes stroking his fine hair until his eyelids drooped shut. When she went looking for Melissa, thinking they might color together or swing on the rope swing in the backyard, she found the child in the old woman's bedroom. The two heads, one white and one golden, were bent together over a small loom that the old woman used to make multicolored hot pads; the kitchen was full of them. They were both absorbed, the bony old hands expertly threading a shuttle in and out while the dimpled baby fingers pushed the yarn up against the already-finished work.

Joanne turned back into the kitchen, looking around for something to occupy herself. There was nothing to do; the wash wouldn't be dry enough to bring in yet. She sighed once, quietly, and then strode out into the still-brisk spring wind, heading quickly for the low door at the side of the barn. Even before she reached for the latch, she noticed that there were no cheeping sounds coming from the other side of the door, and a sudden prickly feeling spread up her neck and into the back of her head. She pulled the door open and stepped inside all in one motion.

The floor and lower walls were dotted and smeared with blood. Tiny bodies were strewn everywhere, their feathers wet and matted. Only two chicks remained on their feet, swaying, too much in shock from their wounds to make any sound. The heat lamps were swinging slowly back and forth, spotlighting first one corpse and then another. Crouched against the far wall in a corner behind the overturned water trough was an orange-and-white striped tomcat, the blood on his mouth and whiskers making him look as if he were smiling. He turned his yellow eyes up at Joanne, a slow, blank look that seemed to see through her to the open door behind.

For perhaps twenty seconds, Joanne looked back and forth over the little room, her mouth agape, air held in her lungs. Then she snapped her jaw shut and pushed the air out between her teeth in a long hissing sound. It seemed to her that the edges of her mind were darkening, moving inward toward the center like a camera lens, until she focused only on the cat, his bloody smirk and his yellow eyes.

Gently, so as not to alarm him, she closed the door behind her, turned the tunnel of her vision over the walls looking for the opening through which the cat must have got into the room. It was just to her left, a hole about four feet above the floor, a gap between the planks that opened into the barn. It must have been a tight squeeze, for the cat was large. Deliberately, Joanne placed her back against the hole, her mind racing. How, how to kill him? She distrusted the strength of her own hands, feared the cat would scratch himself free if she followed her first impulse to strangle him. Frank had a gun in the barn, a 22 caliber rifle, but she didn't know how to make it work; besides, the cat was sure to get away if she left the room. She looked down at the floor even before she remembered the half-empty sack she'd set down next to the door that morning.

Moving slowly and carefully, Joanne stooped to gather the sack into her left hand, never taking her eyes from the cat, which still crouched in the same spot. She removed the twine and poured the ground feed onto the floor. She was panting slightly, a shallow breathing that made very little sound. In her stooped movement across the floor, she stepped on one of the dead chicks, but she didn't look down at it. When she reached her right hand toward the cat, he flattened himself further toward the floor and, twisting his face up at her, hissed sharply.

Joanne used the moment of warning to lunge at the fur behind the cat's head. He struggled violently, doubling himself up and kicking out with all four legs as Joanne lifted him, but she had a handful of fur and skin, and she merely tightened her grip. The cat raked his claws across her left forearm as she maneuvered the twitching body into the sack. Then she carried the struggling weight to the door and twisted the twine firmly around the top of the sack, pausing only a second to wipe away the blood that was welling up in the center of her worst scratches.

Outside, Joanne leaned against the building, pulling great mouthfuls of air into her lungs, holding the bag away from her body as the struggling and snarling inside began to subside. The center of her mind was quite calm, casting about at an almost leisurely pace for a method of killing the cat now that he couldn't escape. She'd heard that people sometimes drowned kittens in a sack. Only ten steps from her was the big water tank where the cows drank when they were in the yard. But she rejected this almost immediately. If she put the sack into the tank, she'd have to stand there waiting, and her muscles ached to do something.

At last, Joanne's swinging gaze fell on the pickup parked next to the machine shed; it was the same truck in which she and Frank had gone to the movies when they were dating, and it was still their only means of transportation. Joanne closed her mouth firmly and walked out onto the graveled driveway that swept from the road to the barn doors. The cat had stopped struggling and lay quietly at the bottom of the bag, but when Joanne set it down in the center of the driveway, he began to writhe again. She checked to see that the twine was securely knotted and then dropped the top of the sack.

The truck took a while starting, the ignition grinding as it always did when the engine was cold. When it finally coughed into life, Joanne revved the motor six or seven times, taking satisfaction in the thrust of her leg against the gas pedal and in the roaring sound of the old engine. She put in the clutch and shifted into low, pulling the floor-mounted shift lever with all the strength of her right arm. The truck lurched forward and Joanne steered carefully so that the right wheels would go over the sack. As soon as she could feel that this had happened, she stamped on the clutch and brake simultaneously, and slammed the shift lever into reverse.

Back and forth she went, never so far backward that she could see the sack, expending tremendous energy in working the pedals and shift lever, her mind numb and washed to blankness by the physical exertion. She lost count of the times she went forward and backward. At first the wheels bumped up and down over the bag, but eventually there was only the smooth motion, a rhythmically hypnotizing roar of engine and gears. Finally, Joanne's arm began to ache. She backed the truck up to the machine shed and turned it off; then she slid to the ground and strode into the house without once looking behind her.

Melissa and the old woman were huddled together just inside the kitchen. When Joanne slammed the door, the blind woman threw up her hands, clawing the air in a gesture of fear.

"What is it?" she quavered. "Who's there?"

"It's me," Joanne snapped. "Stand out of my way."

"I heard the truck," the old woman shouted. "What were you doing?"

"Nothing to do with you," Joanne said, brushing past her mother-in-law, deliberately bumping the tiny old body so that the blind woman had to clutch at a chair to steady herself.

"Go outside and see what Mama was doing," the old woman said to Melissa.

Halfway across the room, Joanne spun around, her rage boiling up in her again.

"You stay in this house, Melissa," she said in a flat, deadly voice.

The child's eyes became even wider and she turned her pale face into the old woman's stomach. Joanne felt a constriction around her heart, sudden tears on her face.

"I'm going to take a bath," she said harshly and fled from the kitchen.

She let about four inches of water into the old, footed bathtub and threw off her clothes. Not even the scratches on her arm seemed to have any feeling as she scrubbed herself all over with the cheap soap she always bought four bars at a time. Standing, she rubbed her skin red with a stiff bath towel and stepped out onto the tiles. She felt calmer now, as if her energy were swirling down the drain with the bathwater. Once out of the warmth of the bathroom, she realized that she was exhausted, could not summon the strength to put clothes on her body. She stood naked in the middle of the bedroom, her arms hanging limply at her sides, looking around the room as if she didn't recognize it. Finally, she pulled on the frayed chenille bathrobe that hung behind the door and padded barefoot into the kitchen.

Melissa was still clinging to her grandmother, who was sitting in a wooden rocking chair. Joanne sank down onto a chair, propped her elbows on the table, and held her head between her hands. From upstairs, she could hear the baby, not yet crying, but making the noise he used to signal that he wanted to get up. After a moment or two, the old woman spoke.

"Are you going to get the baby?" Her voice was tentative, a little fearful.

"No, I'm not up to it right now," Joanne said in a dull voice. "You can take care of him."

The old woman heard the change in Joanne's voice and was instantly herself again.

"Well, such goings-on," she cried. "Trucks roaring around to wake folks up, and then a baby can't even get his own mother to tend him."

And she bustled out of the room, running her forefinger along the wall to guide herself. After one long look at her mother, Melissa ran after her grandmother, giving the table a wide berth as she passed.

Joanne was still sitting in the same position when Frank came in for lunch twenty minutes later. He walked up behind her slowly, cautiously, looking around the room as he moved. When she didn't stir or look up, he stopped, folded his arms, and pursed his mouth.

"What's that mess on the driveway?" he asked.

Then Joanne looked up at him and he fell back a pace or two from the expression on her face. For another long moment, he looked at her, blinking and frowning slightly. Then he went back outside.

Another fifteen minutes passed and Joanne didn't move her head. Her eyes took in the back door, the row of clothes hooks, the faded wallpaper, the clock with its cord trailing along the wall to an outlet, but none of it registered in her mind. Finally, she began to hear a faint scratching sound from outside in the yard. A little wave of panic raced over her otherwise numbed feelings. For a second, she thought the cat might be alive, scratching his way out of the bag.

Reason reasserted itself immediately. She stood up, pushing herself erect with both hands against the tabletop, and walked to the kitchen window. In the middle of the driveway stood the wheelbarrow with a shovel faceup across it. Frank was bent over next to the wheelbarrow, raking a fresh mound of gravel, scratching the rake back and forth to smooth the stones level with the driveway. In that posture, Joanne thought, he looked shapeless, old.

Lee Ann's Little Killing

(1971)

The three-year-old watched her older sister with the wide, seemingly vacant stare that very young children often have. Then, just as the older girl turned to lift a box, the baby dived at the neatly arranged piles of paper doll clothes, coming away with a bright wad of paper in her left hand.

"You stop that!" the seven-year-old cried, making a well-practiced grab at the blond curls across from her.

The baby screamed fiercely, holding the crumpled doll clothes against her stomach as the older girl tried to get hold of the clenched fist without letting go of the curls.

"Let go of her this instant!" a woman's voice cut into the noise.

Both children were silenced for a few seconds, looking up at the thin figure in the dining room doorway. Then the baby began to wail piteously, squirming to free her head and reaching up with her free arm toward her mother.

"Lee Ann Krieger, let go of that child's hair," the woman said, separating each of the last six words with a tiny pause.

"She's grabbing my paper dolls," Lee Ann said, but she released the baby, who jumped up from the floor where they'd both been sitting. She was lifted up into her mother's arms, still hiding the paper clothes against her body.

"You should know better than to fight with Julie. She's only a baby," the mother said without looking at Lee Ann, but stroking the baby's head.

"She's not such a baby," Lee Ann said, pulling scattered doll things toward herself. "And she's still got some clothes, there in her hand."

"What do you have in your hand, Baby? Show Mama." The mother's voice had softened to a cajoling, soothing tone.

The baby pulled her hand out from between her mother's body and her own, opened her dimpled fingers, and let the crumpled paper fall to the floor. Lee Ann looked at the wad without making any move to touch it. Tears stung her eyes, blurring the bright colors into a moving wash.

"They're all wrecked," she said, looking up at her mother.

"I don't want to hear any more about it," the woman said. "If you don't want your sister getting into your things, you shouldn't spread them out all over the dining room floor. Now clean up this mess."

For another moment, the child looked up at the familiar picture, Julie held high against her mother's face and shoulder. When Lee Ann thought about her mother's face, she often pictured this angle, the features foreshortened above her, the muscles moving under the jaw as her mother spoke. Lee Ann pursed her own mouth tight shut and began gathering paper dolls into the box.

"What's the problem here?" another, deeper voice said from above her. The child's eyes flew up to the sun-reddened face that was now beside her mother's. Tears started fresh in her eyes, but she said nothing.

"The usual," the woman sighed as she turned to carry the snuffling baby into the kitchen.

The man squatted down in the doorway, bringing his face level with his kneeling daughter. He had thick, carrot-colored hair, blue eyes, and patches of freckles on either side of his nose.

"Come on, Skippy," he said softly. "Cheer up. I'm done with my newspaper now, and you and me are going out to make some fence this side of the woods. How about it?"

"Okay," she said, wiping the palms of her hands under both eyes.

In the large, airy kitchen, the man said to his wife, "I'm taking Lee Ann out to make fence with me. We should be back about four, four-thirty."

"Fine, fine," the wife answered as she piled lunch dishes into the sink. The baby was licking the last of the vanilla pudding out of a large plastic bowl.

"Now you mind your dad and try to stay out of his way," the mother said, turning briefly to Lee Ann. "And be careful to sit still on the tractor." She turned to her husband to add, "Roy, you see to it that you're both careful out there." All of this was said without rancor, automatically, and no response was called for, a good thing since Lee Ann was still feeling too sore to speak to her mother.

Outside the back door, the early summer sun bathed the farmyard and the outbuildings in a cool light; the lawn still had the yellowish green hue of new grass. Lee Ann's father said she had to wear her windbreaker, but she didn't have to zip it. He wore his denim jacket and a baseball cap. The tractor was parked at the side of the barn. It was an old but clean Oliver 88, its dark green paint making it look bravely cheerful against the weathered barn boards. Lee Ann couldn't remember a time when the tractor hadn't been familiar to her, more familiar than the family car, for she'd been riding around on the tractor ever since she was "a little bitty Skippy," as her father said.

She sat in the driver's seat in front of her father, leaning forward with both hands on the spokes of the steering wheel, helping him to drive. As the tractor moved out toward the cow lane, Lee Ann glanced back toward the house. The blue-and-white striped awnings over the two front windows always made the child think that the house looked sleepy, its eyelids half-closed, the door yawning widely between. Inside, she knew, her mother was getting Julie ready for her nap, stripping off her shoes and socks, playing "This little piggy went to market" with her toes. Lee Ann turned her face away from the house toward the cow lane, breathing deeply the rich fuel smell of the tractor. This was where she felt most at home, in the air, among the farm machines, with her father's knees against her sides.

When the tractor rounded the machine shed and could no

longer be seen from the house, Lee Ann's father said into her ear, "I'm gonna stand in back, okay?"

She turned her face to him, nodding vigorously and grinning. This was a special treat, one she knew must be their secret, never talked about in front of Mama. Her father would stand up with the tractor still moving, swing his leg backward off the seat, and climb down onto the lower platform of the tractor. He would hold onto the seat and let Lee Ann drive. The tractor moved slowly—he had throttled it down—and the lane was straight, without ditches. Still, there was a special rule when Lee Ann drove the tractor; while her father could talk to her, she must not look around or try to talk to him; with her face forward, he couldn't hear her anyway. Occasionally, his right hand would come past her to correct the tractor's direction, but she was getting pretty good at keeping to a straight line. They crept along toward the woods, which they could see across the center of the horizon.

After a while, her father said, "A baby can sometimes be a pest, huh?"

She nodded sharply several times.

"But they don't know as much as big girls," he went on, "so we have to take care to keep things out of their way."

She nodded again, but more slowly.

When they got to the pasture he climbed back to the seat, braked the tractor to a stop next to a canvas-covered pile of fence posts, and turned off the engine. Lee Ann helped him to fold up the canvas sheet, exposing the narrow steel posts with their sharpened ends all pointing in the same direction toward a long piece of twine stretched just above the grass.

"Why do we need a fence here, Daddy?" she asked as he lifted a sledgehammer from the center of the pile.

"Well, I got this pasture cleared and worked for the cows," he said, sweeping his arm from left to right over the newly sprouted clover, "and we gotta keep them from wandering off into the woods. You remember when there were trees all through here, don't you?"

She nodded, but she didn't really remember the trees. Grownups could always remember things from longer ago, she knew, so they thought she could remember too. Her father stood leaning on the sledgehammer, looking at her for such a long time that she began to feel uncomfortable.

"You know, Lee Ann," he said at last—he always called her Lee Ann when he meant to be very serious. "Your mama doesn't mean a lot of what she says."

"She always takes Julie's side," she said quickly. "She acts like she doesn't even hear what I say."

"Well, she spends all her time with the baby," he said, "cuz babies need lots of taking care of, so she seems to understand Julie better."

In her mind, Lee Ann finished the thought, "And that's why she doesn't love me." Out loud, she said, "The same way she always had to take care of Jeff?" speaking the name fearfully, knowing from long experience how its sound seemed to affect her parents.

Her father let go of the sledgehammer, which stood poised for a second before falling over, and then came over to squat next to her.

"Yes, Jeff is a big part of it," he said quietly, looking up at her. She could see her own face reflected in the center of both his eyes. "You were so little when he first got sick, only two, and that was a time when Mama should have always been with you. But she got all tied up in Jeff's being so sick, in trying to help him get better, and you just naturally started being more with me, doing things with me outside because there had to be quiet in the house. And then Julie was born just after he died." And again, Lee Ann thought that the unspoken rest of the speech was, "And that's why she loves Julie better." She thought this without bitterness, just as a fact which could be explained like other facts.

He put his square, freckled hand on her arm, and Lee Ann looked down at it, noting with satisfaction its well-fleshed solidity, its ruddy color.

"Your mama loves you," he said, as if answering her thought. "She just doesn't know how you're thinking, and she expects that you understand lots of things now that you're finished with the first grade and everything."

She nodded without looking up, and he patted her arm clumsily.

"Now you stay back here by the tractor while I'm pounding posts," he said, standing up. "No creeping up on me now, cuz it's dangerous."

Lee Ann sat down against the tractor's rear wheel while her father paced off along the twine from the last post he'd driven into the ground the day before. He set a post up and, holding the sledgehammer high on the handle, his hand only about four inches from the head, tapped the end of the post until the sharp end had sunk into the ground. Then he stood back, grasped the handle near the end, and swung the sixteen-pound hammer in a wide arc over his head, making a loud grunting sound just before the head crashed onto the post. Lee Ann thought the pounding made a sound like a bell, the tone changing with each swing of the hammer. She watched her father's back and well-muscled arms.

He hadn't seemed upset this time when she mentioned Jeff. Maybe he was beginning to forget, or maybe it was just that she hadn't said the name in front of Mama. Lee Ann could hardly remember her brother at all. She'd been only four when he died, so what she remembered was her parents' response, what they and other grownups said about Jeff. Her father had tried to help her, over the years, to understand why it wasn't just old people who died. Some children got sick, he said, like Mr. Himrich's one son who had died of a fever, years ago now, when he was just a little boy. And Sharon Tomchek who sang in the choir with him—her older brother was killed in a car accident, and he wasn't even twenty yet when it happened. And these were people she knew, he reminded her.

Jeff had been sick a long time with something called leukemia, a word that Lee Ann kept in her mind as the name for all bad sicknesses, a terrible word that grownups said in a whisper. Whenever she had a stomach pain or an earache, she thought of the word and felt she couldn't tell anyone because her mother would start to look the way she looked whenever that sickness was mentioned. Lee Ann had to get a shot for an earache once because, the doctor said, she hadn't told about it soon enough.

And it would be hard for her to remember Jeff because he'd spent so much time in the hospital, a place so terrible that only grownups were allowed to go there to visit. Her mother had gone every day while she stayed with her father, in the barn, in the fields, in his basement workshop, going into Hammern with him to the mill. But she did have one memory of Jeff, an image so clear that she could close her eyes any time and see it as if it were right in front of her. Just before he went back to the hospital for the last time, she had climbed up onto his bed in the sunny ground-floor room that her mother now used as a sewing room. It was not his face that she remembered—it was only photographs that formed her impression of what his face had looked like. She remembered his hands, both of them lying on top of the bed covers, sticking out at the ends of his peppermint-striped pajama sleeves. The hands were bluish white and so thin that the skin looked stretched tight over the bones of his fingers and wrists. They looked smaller than her own hands even though he was three years older. The hands made Lee Ann think of the paper skeleton her father hung on the outside door on Halloween.

And that was why she watched her father's hands. In church on Sundays, she went into the pew first, followed by her father, then Julie, then her mother. They had to turn back toward the altar to watch the priest, the whole family looking away from Lee Ann, and this gave her a chance to watch her father without anyone knowing. So at least once a week she could spend some time measuring his hands when he wasn't using them to work, checking to see if they were still wide, still reddish brown. Sometimes, she would reach out and spread her own hand over one of his to reassure herself that the relative size remained as it

Winter Roads, Summer Fields

should be. He would turn and smile at her, but her mother, noticing the motion, would frown for her to sit up and pay attention.

When her father had pounded three posts, he came to sit next to her in the shade of the tractor wheel.

"I'm working up a sweat," he said, panting slightly.

They sat side by side looking out past his work toward a neighboring set of farm buildings: a bright red barn, two dark blue silos reflecting the afternoon sun like great round mirrors, a third silo almost half-built, with the moving shapes of workmen faintly visible along its upper edge.

"Why do the Ihnefelds need three silos when we have only one?" Lee Ann asked dreamily.

"Well, Marvin keeps buying more land and more cows," he said. "Guess he has to have a place to keep all that feed."

"Why does he keep doing that?"

"You're full of hard questions, aren't you? I don't know. He likes work, maybe. Most likely, he's thinking about getting enough work for his boys. He wants enough to keep them busy and to leave to them when he goes. He's got those three boys."

Lee Ann looked up at him, hearing the change in his voice. He was looking out over his newly cleared field.

"When he goes where?" Lee Ann said.

"I don't know," he said, rubbing the top of her head with his knuckles. "When he goes to Cleveland."

"What's Cleveland?"

"Skippy is a Question Box," he chanted, laughing loudly.

"I can help you with all your work when I get bigger," she said after a while.

"You help me right now," he said softly. "A lot."

"Can we get a blue silo?"

"Maybe someday. Right now I have to get some wire hooks set into those posts. You open the toolbox on the tractor and get ready to fetch me the tools I'll need, okay?"

Lee Ann's Little Killing

"Sure thing," she said, jumping up and pulling on his thumbs to raise him.

"First you can bring me the pliers," he called to her from the post. She trotted over to him with the tool and then stood watching as he pushed a short piece of double-twisted wire halfway through a hole near the top of the post, using the pliers to separate the strands on the other side and bend them around the edges of the post.

When he'd done this in a second hole farther down the post, he said to her, "Run over and throw me the hammer so I can pound these ends nice and snug against the post. This is tough wire."

She ran to the toolbox to find the hammer. He had said for her to throw it, and she was glad for the chance to show off this skill. Sometimes she played softball with her father, and he always admired the way she could throw a ball. Once she'd heard him tell Grandpa Krieger that she could throw like a boy. She hefted the hammer in her hand, judging the distance to a spot near her father's feet. Then she leaned back the way the pitchers on television did and threw overhand, calling, "Here, Daddy!"

He was squatting, working with the pliers on the second hook, and he lifted his head to look in her direction. The hammer had turned over twice in the air, whirling in a much higher arc than Lee Ann had intended, and now the hammer head struck the brim of his baseball cap, crushing through it to the center of his forehead. It made a thudding sound that Lee Ann could hear where she was standing about fifteen feet away. He rolled straight over backwards, with his knees, still bent from his squat, lifting up into the air. Then his legs slowly straightened and fell to the ground.

The child stood frozen, her arm still extended from the follow-through of the throw.

"Daddy?" she called.

No sound, no movement came from the fallen man.

Lee Ann began to walk toward him, first calling, then

whimpering, "Daddy? Daddy?" over and over again. Just before she could see his face, she pinched her eyes tightly shut and took one more long step. Maybe if you didn't see things, they weren't real; if you didn't look at them, they would go away, would never have happened in the first place. But she forced her eyes open and looked down at her father's face.

He was facing straight up at the sky, his eyes were shut in a hard frown, and the cap had fallen off just behind his head. Across his forehead was a wide gash, and the coppery red of his hair lent, by contrast, a bluish cast to the glistening red of the blood which had already soaked his hair all the way to the crown of his head. His hands, looking almost white against the dark earth, lay palm up on either side of his face.

Lee Ann turned and began to run. By the time she reached the lane, the tears had started, followed by a convulsive sobbing that caused a twisting pain in her stomach. She ran as fast as she could, not thinking about where she was running or why, for the sounds of her tennis shoes beating against the packed earth kept time with the two words in her mind: "He's dead he's dead he's dead he's dead."

It was a half-mile to the farm buildings, and before she'd gone halfway the combined effort of running and sobbing had so affected her breathing that there was a roaring in her head, a roaring that began to form rhythmic words, "I killed him, I killed him, I killed him." But she kept up almost the same pace. Once, after she'd fallen and scrambled up again, the thought passed through her mind that the wound on her father's head had a name, was called something that her mind turned from until there was only the roaring again.

She rounded the machine shed, staggered across the cow yard, her feet sinking into the urine-soaked ground, and scrambled under the fence that separated the cow yard from the lawn. She was halfway to the house before she noticed her mother hanging dish towels on the wash lines. She stopped in her tracks, swaying dangerously as if the impetus of her forward motion would make her fall onto her face on the graveled driveway.

Her mother's face, wide-eyed and open-mouthed, came into focus, moving toward her in slow motion. At first the roaring in Lee Ann's head made it impossible to hear what her mother was saying; there was only a moving mouth opening and closing like the mouths on television when the sound was off. Finally, words began to come into Lee Ann's mind.

"What's the matter? Where's your dad?" The face above Lee Ann was turned toward the fields, searching the horizon. Tears began again in the child's eyes, and her mother's face blurred before it could turn back to her, blurred so that its expression couldn't be defined. But the words went on in a hurried, breathy voice.

"Did he have an accident with the tractor? Did the tractor turn over?"

Lee Ann was still gasping for breath, sobbing even as she tried to draw air into her lungs, so she couldn't speak. But also, in the deepest part of her mind, she felt that she must not speak, must not say the words that the roaring had said. If she said it out loud, the saying would make it true, make it real. If she didn't speak, it would all be just a dream; it would go away like the stomach pains that might be called leukemia if you told anyone about them, that might *become* leukemia if you could be made to say, "My tummy hurts."

Now her mother touched her for the first time since she'd come into the yard, putting a hand on either shoulder and shaking the child sharply.

"Talk to me! Say something! Why did you run home like that? What's happened to Daddy?" Her mother was beginning to breathe hard, as if she'd been running too.

Lee Ann began to shake her head back and forth. She was beginning to hear her own sobs now. Suddenly another sound began to intrude above the heaving of her chest. She stopped her head only to notice that her mother had heard the other noise first and had let go of her shoulders to take a step toward the cow yard. It was the sound of the tractor, a high-pitched, almost hysterical putt-putting that the tractor made only when it was being driven in high gear.

Mother and daughter stood transfixed as the tractor came into view around the machine shed, its hatless driver bouncing up and down in the seat as the tractor sped across the cow yard. At the fence, it stopped with a snorting shudder. Neither Lee Ann nor her mother moved forward, rooted to the tidy yard as the man opened the wire gate, closed it behind him, and started up toward them. In his right hand, he carried a large handkerchief, one of those with his initials on it; the handkerchief was smeared with blood. As he got closer, they could see that his forehead was swollen and cut, but it was no longer bleeding. Only when he was within five feet of them did the woman spring forward to close the distance between herself and her husband.

Lee Ann didn't really hear what they said to each other because, inside her mind, there was room for only one set of words: "I didn't say it. I did right not to say it. I made it not true by not saying it. Thank you, God, that I didn't say it." Her heart was bursting with gratitude that he had been given back to her, brought back from the dead like those holy people Sister Margaret told them about at school.

Her parents turned to her now, took a few steps in her direction. Then the mother stopped again with her arms folded tightly across her chest and looked out over the fields. Her father came the rest of the way to her, standing straight up above her, looking down as he spoke. His voice was strange, cold.

"That was not a good thing to do, Lee Ann. Throwing heavy things is very dangerous, and you should know that. When I say 'Throw me the hammer,' I mean for you to bring it to me."

She didn't speak but reached out to take his hand in both of hers. She looked up at his head which, at this angle, looked miles above her, level with the barn roof and glowing fiery red in the sun. The swollen forehead jutted forward like a bulge on a mountain, the dried blood dark, almost black, against his skin.

"And you shouldn't have run away so fast," he was saying, the muscles under his jaw working. "I was only stunned. I could hear you calling me, but I couldn't answer or even move for the life of me. By the time I could sit up, you were so far away I couldn't call to you."

She looked down with tears starting on her face again, looked at his hand, square and dark as ever, her own hands on either side of it looking tiny and pale.

"Now I know that you'll never do something like that again," he said. "If you're going to be my helper, you have to be careful around tools and machines."

Her tears were falling onto his hand, running down onto the thick fingers. He didn't pull his hand away, but he didn't squeeze her fingers either. She had forgotten everything—about Julie, about leukemia. She didn't care where her mother was standing. Nothing else on earth mattered except that he should forgive her, let her go on the tractor with him, call her Skippy, bend down to her again.

Winter Roads, Summer Fields

Mass for the Dead

(1977)

He sat so straight that no part of his spine touched the back of the metal folding chair. His body, still immature at fourteen, gave no more shape to his suit than a coat hanger would have. Under a fringe of blond hair that came almost to his eyes, his face was set in stubborn anger, a mixture of indignation and resentment that stiffened the childish lines of his jaw, making him look older than his years.

It was the morning of his mother's funeral, and the public room where her body was displayed was filled with whispering people who moved softly through the heavily perfumed air. The family was gathered around the casket for the final farewell, but the crowd and the movement made it possible for the boy's separateness to go unnoticed. He was watching the back of his father's head. In the center of the tableau, the father knelt, bent almost double and shaking with sobs. Weak, the boy thought. Always demanding, always so sure he was right, but in the end just weak. Yes, somebody was to blame, and the boy had taken it upon himself to see to it that justice was paid out. He was making his plans.

"Todd!" His sister, Elaine, surprised him; he hadn't seen her move. "Come up here right now. You could at least stop acting like this when everybody's around. Don't you know they're going to close the coffin in a minute, and you'll never see Mama again?"

And she began to cry again, lifting a mascara-stained handkerchief to her mouth and reaching behind herself for her fiancé's hand. The boy stood up without a word and walked to stand directly behind their older brother. Bob was tall, over six feet, and the boy could stare at the shoulders of his striped jacket.

He wouldn't look at his mother's body again. He'd done so only once, yesterday morning. Her small face was frozen into an expressionless mask; it must have been hard to smooth out the distortions that had marred it the last few hours it was a living face. Her pale hair, which she'd always worn loose around her face and skimming her shoulders, was now piled high on her head and set in a puffy cluster of curls. Party curls, they were called, he remembered. After that one look, he'd moved his eyes to her hands, folded on the lilac-colored gown she'd made to wear to Elaine's wedding. At least the hands were still his mother's hands; the mole on her right thumb still showed through the makeup. He'd wanted to touch her hands, but he was afraid.

Once, when he was eight, his parents had taken him to a wax museum in Chicago while they were visiting his father's sister. There was one grouping with George Washington extending his arm toward raggedly dressed soldiers. The figure was close to the velvet rope, and it was fascinatingly lifelike. Todd had waited until the rest of the family moved ahead, and then, by leaning far over the swaying rope, he had touched George Washington's hand with his own right hand. The cold, slightly oily wax sent a shiver straight up the boy's arm and into his body. He'd run in a kind of panic to catch up to his mother, reaching for her hand with his still-clean left hand. While his father's voice rang in the hollowed rooms—"For heaven's sake, don't hang on your mother. You're eight years old, not a baby"—he'd rubbed his right hand against his pants, over and over. Chicago was only a confused blur in his memory, but he'd never forgotten George Washington's hand. Suppose his mother's dead hand were to feel like that? He couldn't take the chance, and he wouldn't look at her again.

Instead, he watched his grandmother. Standing at the foot of the casket, she never took her eyes from the face of her dead child. It struck the boy that it must seem odd to Grandma to stand here surrounded by her grandchildren and even great-grandchildren— Bob's two children, confused and subdued by the scene, fidgeted nearby—facing the death of her own daughter. Her eighty years had shrunk her and toughened her; she'd buried her husband with calm resignation, but she was suddenly shaken into an old

Winter Roads, Summer Fields

woman's tremor by this loss. The boy thought it was odd too, and he wished with all his heart that the normal thing had happened, that his grandmother were in the casket and his mother grieving in her place.

No one was paying attention to him now, and Mr. Steiner, the funeral director, was already murmuring to them that they must leave the room for "the closing." The funeral mass was to begin promptly at ten and the drive to the church would be slow. Their father stood up; Carol, Bob's wife, had to help him. He rested his hands on the edge of the casket for just a second and then softly, as if he was afraid he would wrinkle it, touched the sleeve of his wife's dress. They all filed out then with the father leading them.

The family waiting room was small, full of dark green velvet, and was separated from the larger funeral parlor by only a curtain. A complete hush had fallen over the people in the big room, and the boy knew Mr. Steiner must be folding the crinkled satin panels over his mother's face. Would the coffin cover push those panels into her face, he wondered, or just clear her nose so that the panels would be like a veil? The sound of the casket closing was so distinct that they all jumped with the shock of it. It sounded like the door closing on a well-made car. You get what you pay for— that's what his father always said about cars. Trucks and tractors, too. Margaret, the boy's other sister, said something to her young husband, Tony; her veiled face leaned toward him and the black net moved faintly, but Todd couldn't hear what she said.

Suddenly the curtain swept back, and everyone jumped again. Mr. Steiner directed them to the outside doors where the funeral procession was parked. Now there was a moment of confusion, for no one had planned the seating arrangements in the cars. Bob took over at once.

"Todd, you and Grandma ride with Papa in the first car."

"No." He could tell by Bob's frown that he'd spoken too quickly. "Let Elaine and Frank go with him and Grandma. You and Carol and the kids can go in the second car, and I'll ride with Margaret and Tony. It comes out more even that way."

He'd planned this out ahead of time; he would sit in the second pew of the church, not with his father. Bob looked suspicious, but there was no time for an argument, so they moved outside in the boy's suggested order.

Their bodies received the double shock of the lung-biting February cold and the sunlight glaring off the roofs of parked cars and mounds of newly shoveled snow. All the cars had their headlights on, feeble competition for that mid-morning winter sunshine. The only unusual vehicles were the hearse and, in front of it with lights flashing, a county police car. The rest of the procession consisted of the family cars of friends and relatives, taken through the only enclosed car wash yesterday and driven by their owners.

The boy knew about the car wash because his father had driven for Leonard Johnson's funeral the summer before. The afternoon before that funeral, Todd's mother was baking furiously, despite the 90-degree heat — two fancy cakes for the funeral meal. She'd looked up when Todd and her husband came in from the fields, covered with dust and chaff.

"You should clean up and take the car over to Cyrus's," she said, passing a towel under her chin where the perspiration was collecting. The man had only sighed for answer, pulling off his sweat-stained shirt and draping it over a hook in the back hallway.

"Why should the car be clean?" the boy asked.

His mother's quick answer had been: "We show our respect for the dead and the family that way, Todd."

"And, of course, it wouldn't do for us to have the only dirty car in the parade," the father had chuckled.

"Now, George! Don't put such ideas in the boy's head." She'd turned sharply back to them and was trying to look angry, but suddenly she and her husband had smiled at each other, one of those secret smiles that the boy was just then beginning to hate.

So now the clean cars were turning out for her. It was like

everything else that had happened in the past four days. Without ever planning for it or requesting it, the members of the immediate family had simply been relieved of routine duties. Food appeared, cleaning and tidying happened, chores got done. From the living room, the family could occasionally hear, without really noticing, the faint sounds of aunts and neighbors moving and murmuring in the kitchen two rooms away. Men in overalls moved quietly in and out for meals at dawn and nightfall.

And on this morning of the funeral, Todd found himself sitting in the back of Tom Sensbauer's station wagon, noticing with faint surprise that it was warm; Mr. Sensbauer must have been out here with the motor running for quite some time. Margaret sat against Tony, her face obscured by the veil which allowed no one except her husband to see her emotion. Todd needed no veil to hide his emotions; the muscles of his face had settled into his present mask from the morning after his mother's death when no one would listen to him. He'd tried to tell them, but nobody would understand, so it was not his fault. When he would finally reveal the secret, no one could blame him.

They'd gathered in the living room to talk about the arrangements, all except Elaine, who'd been given a sedative and was still resting. Bob, as the eldest, was trying to take the burden from his father's shoulders.

"Pa, listen. I'll go down to Steiner's after lunch and talk to him about everything. You won't have to be there. I'll pick out— whatever is needed."

The father lifted his face, his puffy eyelids making him look sleepy.

"The best, Bob. She's got to have the best. Nothing cheap. And tell Steiner to fix—to try to make her face look nice."

"I know, Pa. Don't worry. Steiner's good. He's done harder things. What should I take for her to wear?"

The father lifted his arms and looked pleadingly around the room. Such matters had always been outside his notice, even his comprehension.

Mass for the Dead

93

"The new dress," Margaret said in a dull voice. "She must have finished it last week. You know Mama—always has to have things done a month in advance."

Her use of the present tense and her reminder of Elaine's wedding closed every throat in the room for a few minutes. When Bob spoke again, it was almost in a whisper.

"If you know where it is, Margaret, get it for me after lunch. Now, Pa, Father Schmidt is expecting us at three to talk about the cemetery plot. I'll be back from Steiner's by then and we can go together to pick it out. Steiner will take care of putting the vault in the ground; that's automatic."

"It should be a double plot, you know." He said it with some surprise, as if it had just occurred to him.

"I know, Pa. I know."

"What about the stone?"

"That comes later. We don't have to think about that now. What kind, what to put on it—that takes some thinking."

There was a long silence, and Todd, who'd been waiting for this chance, spoke at last in the voice that was just beginning to change.

"This is all wrong, you know."

They all turned to the window seat where he was bracing himself on his hands, swaying nervously on stiffened arms.

"Mama never wanted anything like this. She hated this kind of thing."

"What are you talking about?" his father demanded; then, turning to the others, "What's he talking about?"

The boy spoke quickly, afraid of interruptions.

"She should be buried in a plain box without any—any fixing. She wouldn't want anyone looking at her. And why should she be put in a vault too? I don't think there's any law that says she has to be." He saw Bob scowling and getting ready to talk, so he raced on. "I know how she would feel about this because she told me."

"Are you crazy?" His father's nerves were beginning to give

way, and he was shouting, waving his arms in the way that the boy hated. "Is he crazy?"

"I'm telling you, I know what she would want now."

"How the hell would you know anything?" The man was at the edge of hysteria. "You think I'm going to bury her like some bum put away by the county? She's going to have nothing but the best. People are not going to say that I didn't give my wife the best."

"Okay, Pa, okay." Bob was trying to head off the explosion he knew was building in his father. "You stay out of this, Todd. We're going to take care of this the way we planned. Pa, calm down. He's just a kid, and this is hard on all of us. Come on now, Pa. I'm going to see Steiner after lunch, and it's going to be the best."

Todd had slumped back against the wide, old-fashioned window joist, his eyes gone blank. So they wouldn't listen. His father never listened, but even Bob had shut him out, called him a kid, when only he knew. So the boy could do nothing, and when he finally told them everything, it would not be his fault that it was too late. He had tried.

After that he'd said little, sitting pale and dry-eyed while the bustle went on around him. No one bothered him or even paid him much attention, until the day before the funeral when Elaine had suddenly turned on him, her face red and ugly from crying.

"What's the matter with you, anyway? You don't cry. You don't even talk. Say something, for God's sake!"

"Let him alone," Bob said shortly. Impressed as she always was by her older brother, Elaine fell silent. She was only twenty and Frank was probably too young to be much comfort.

And the boy *did* wonder sometimes about his own inability to cry. He felt physically sick most of the time, as if he'd eaten something rotten, and his head felt numb and cold, but he wasn't aware of feeling sad. Bob didn't cry either, but maybe that was because he had no time; he was running everything and having to comfort others all at once. Once or twice Todd found his father

Mass for the Dead

looking at him, a slight frown between his reddened eyes, but they didn't speak to each other, and the man's eyes would slide away again into some great depth where they didn't seem to focus on anything.

Then at the funeral parlor, relatives and friends kept coming up to the boy, trying to comfort him.

"Poor Todd," said Aunt Marie as she put her arm around his rigid shoulders. She'd come up from Chicago without Uncle Stephen. "But she looks so nice, doesn't she? Doesn't she look nice?"

Against his silence, his refusal to even look up at her, she'd finally faltered and walked away. Even Mrs. Pauly, their nearest neighbor and a nonstop talker, had finally given up on him, though she kept hovering around, prattling to Margaret, supervising the food for the funeral meal.

Now the procession had halted before St. Francis Church, where they'd always belonged; even Grandma had been married in this church, and three of Todd's grandparents were already buried in the wooded cemetery across the road. The pallbearers hurried to the back of the hearse, but there was nothing for them to do because the gleaming casket was slid onto a wheeled dolly and pushed into the church. In a nearby field, a herd of cattle had gathered at the fence to watch, calmly chewing and blowing puffy clouds of breath into the still air.

By the time Todd took his place in the second pew, the casket rested on the old wooden catafalque he'd seen so many times from the altar side when he served mass at weekend funerals. His mother had always felt he should volunteer because he could bicycle to church and because people should never pass up opportunities to do corporal works of mercy. Behind him now the church was slowly filling up with relatives, friends, neighbors, curiosity-seekers—all the same people who always came to funerals and weddings in this church.

His mother had never lived anywhere else. Raised on a farm, she'd married a farmer when she was seventeen. Todd had often held the wedding photograph and marveled over the tiny girl whose blond hair and fragile face made her look no older than himself. For almost thirty years, she'd struggled with the endless work of dairy farming and raising four children. She always took her work seriously and, despite leaving school at sixteen, read insatiably during every spare moment because she believed it was important to be the first teacher to her children—and because she was naturally curious, thoughtful. She respected her husband and never complained about her life. She would never permit her children to say one word against their father; her normally mild eyes would flash and she would say, "He works harder than any of us, and he doesn't complain."

Of course Todd knew this was true, but he was silently convinced that the hard-faced man who drove him was also wearing out his mother. Last year she'd taken a job cooking at the senior high school because there weren't so many midday chores on the farm during fall and winter. Yet supper was on time every night as usual, the old house was always spotless, and his father never went without the big breakfasts he'd come to expect. She only got a little thinner and complained sometimes of headaches.

And what was it for? What was it all for? The boy knew. It was so there could be another silo, more cattle, a new milk cooler. The house never changed; no conveniences appeared there. His mother went on using a wringer washing machine and hanging clothes outside, even in the winter. And why? Bob hadn't become a farmer, and the boy had no intention of competing for the land with that man. He would probably bury them all, anyway. Maybe Frank would take it over some day, if he could find nothing better to do, for he was a younger son of a farmer himself.

A hush had fallen in the church now, and Father Schmidt, the young pastor who'd come only last year, came out into the sanctuary dressed in the white vestments that had replaced the traditional black of funeral masses; he was flanked by four young altar boys, all family relatives. The mass began at once; only at the introit prayer did Father Schmidt make the first reference to the

Mass for the Dead

Winter Roads, Summer Fields

occasion. He hadn't been a priest long enough to rush through the prayers, so he spoke slowly, distinctly: "Let us pray for the soul of our sister, Helen, taken from us so suddenly. May her soul and the souls of all the faithfully departed rest in peace." Two hundred voices murmured, "Amen."

Taken from us so suddenly. No specifics, of course. The obituary had been like that too. "Mrs. George (Helen) Frederick died at St. Vincent's Hospital Tuesday after a short illness." The boy had read it all the way through, down to "survivors include," which ended in his own name, spelled with only one "d." Nowhere was there any public mention of the agony, the horror. How could the editor or this young priest know about those two nights?

Todd had been suddenly awakened at three in the morning by his father's voice shouting up the stairs.

"Todd! Todd!"

Something in his tone brought the boy springing to the top of the stairs before he knew he was out of bed. There, in the light of the bare bulb in the lower hallway, he saw the figures oddly foreshortened by the angle of the steep staircase. His thin hair wildly awry, the father was clutching the mother against his chest, carrying her in both arms like a child. She was wrapped in the floral bedspread that normally lay folded at the foot of their bed during the night.

"Call the hospital, Todd." His father's face was yellowish green, and he was panting as if he'd been running for a long time. "Tell them we're on our way. There's no time for an ambulance. Your mother's had a stroke."

Then he turned and ran with his burden toward the back door; he was barefoot and he left that way, running out into the snow with no shoes on his feet. Elaine, who'd come to the railing, was beginning to moan softly as Todd raced for the phone, leaping three steps at a time and slamming his bony hip into the kitchen counter as he ran.

Bob and Carol came to take them both to the hospital the next morning. Elaine remembered to take her father's shoes and

Mass for the Dead

socks. Margaret and Tony were already there, and Frank met them in the waiting room later. Dr. Anderson was tired but patient, trying to make them understand, to give them hope.

"There's some damage, some paralysis, but if she doesn't have another one, she'll recover. There will be a period of therapy—"

"Wait a minute." The father was bewildered. "What exactly has happened to her? What made it happen?"

Todd understood little of what the doctor said next. His mother had had a "cerebral hemorrhage"; a blood vessel in her head had "ballooned" and burst, causing "temporary damage to vital centers, especially to motor sections of the brain." The cause was "undiagnosed high blood pressure." Dr. Anderson wondered aloud why she hadn't had a checkup in over five years, but then Dr. Anderson didn't know her very well. She wouldn't have seen a doctor unless she cut off a finger or broke a bone. "Waste of time and money," she would say briskly. All that the boy understood was a graphic image Dr. Anderson chose to help illustrate the seriousness and consequences of his mother's condition: "It's as if a tiny bomb went off inside her brain."

Father Schmidt had walked to the lectern now for the homily, and everyone settled into sitting positions, the sounds of groaning wood and rustling clothes slowly subsiding into silence.

"My dear friends in Christ. We gather today to mourn our sister, Helen, and to comfort her family. She was a good woman, a loving wife and mother, a friend to all who knew her. As an officer in the Christian Mothers' Society, she gave of her time to her parish, despite her busy life at home and work. She will be sorely missed."

Todd noticed that Mrs. Pauly across the aisle was weeping into her handkerchief, and other women that he could catch in his peripheral vision were crying too. Wasn't that strange? No one in the family was crying, not even Elaine. They all sat there, numb and unmoved. Why was that? It wasn't that the things the priest was saying were untrue—they were not. It was only that they seemed so meaningless coming out of his mouth, a young man who'd hardly known her and whose repeated references to "our sister" and "Helen" couldn't help but seem strange coming from someone young enough to be her son.

"We must be comforted that her earthly trials are over, that she now rests in the peace of Christ where there is no frustration, no disappointment, no pain."

No pain. The doctor had tried to tell them that before they went in to see her that first afternoon. They would find her face distorted, but that was the paralysis—she was not suffering. She was sedated and could not speak, of course. Nothing, however, could prepare them for the sight. The left side of her face was twisted, her mouth opened and curled into what looked like a snarl. Margaret gasped, and their father sank wordlessly into a chair at the bedside.

Late that afternoon, she had the second stroke, and the doctor said that she'd slipped into a coma. At seven o-clock, he said they'd better send for the priest. Bob had to do it, for his father was frozen, could not be persuaded from the room even for coffee. The family was allowed to stay for the last rites because, of course, there would be no confession. Father Schmidt administered conditional absolution and anointed the body. When he said the concluding blessing, "In the name of the Father and of the Son and of the Holy Spirit," the dying woman's right hand twitched and began to rise. Then her eyes opened and rolled for a second before they found her husband standing at the foot of the bed.

With a terrible struggle over each word, she pronounced in a rattling whisper, "Let—me—be," and then drew a gasping breath that shook the metal-framed bed. Her eyes rolled upward.

Immediately her husband began speaking, extending his arms and gesturing wildly at everybody in the room.

"What does she mean? Why does she tell me to let her be?"

"It's all right, Mr. Frederick." Father Schmidt, obviously shaken, moved toward him, blocking his view of his wife. "She doesn't know what she's saying."

Bob caught one of his father's arms. "Pa, she doesn't mean anything. She doesn't even know us."

By the time they could calm the man down, his wife had taken another rattling breath and died.

But Todd was convinced that *he* knew what she meant by saying "Let me be." Over a year ago, they'd had a long talk after Grandma Frederick's funeral. The others were still at the church hall, but mother and son had come home so she could cook and prepare sleeping room for out-of-town relatives and he could begin chores. He had straddled a chair, grateful for an hour alone with his mother, an hour without duties. She never stopped moving around the large kitchen as she talked.

"You know, Toddy, I don't like these things very much."

"What things?"

"Oh, all of it. The way we do funerals."

"Why not?"

"I can't say it exactly, but it's so—not *real*. Everybody saying Grandma looked nice, but she didn't look anything like herself. You know she never wore makeup, and she *hated* those glasses even though she had to wear them to sew. Didn't it seem funny to have those glasses on her?"

"Yeah, I guess it did." It hadn't occurred to him, but now that she said it, it *did* seem absurd—glasses on dead eyes. His mother was slicing onions onto a roast, holding them as far away from her face as her short arms would permit.

"And all that embalming and everything. It doesn't seem natural, does it? Rose Pauly says it's a law, but I don't know. If a person doesn't have anything *catching*, why should she be disinfected or pickled?"

She paused, and they both giggled softly over the word.

"I don't mean disrespect," she said with a sobered face. "She was your father's mother. But I can't help thinking *their* way isn't very respectful. They paint her all up, put her into a sealed coffin, and then into a cement vault in the ground just so she won't decay. But dead things are *supposed* to decay, aren't they? I mean, it's the way of things. Flesh decomposes when it's dead, so that must be what God *intended*. Maybe it's wrong to interfere in that. Haven't you ever thought about it that way?"

She always talked to him like that, as if he thought things through, had ideas of his own worth listening to. Of course, he agreed with her at once.

"Sure, Mama. But everybody seems to do it this way—like for Grandma. What else could be done?"

The roast was in the oven, and strips of carrot peel were flying into the sink. She paused to pass the back of her hand under her nose.

"Well, Grandma Frederick *herself* told me about her father's funeral—your great-grandfather. He died at home too, just like Grandma, and they washed and dressed his body themselves—his family, I mean—even his own wife. Then Grandma's brother built one of those shaped coffins; six sides it had, I think. He was a carpenter, that brother—Uncle Matt. They had it all done on the same day, and then they put the coffin across six dining room chairs. People came that night and the next day for prayers, and on the third morning, they buried him. Grandma said the coffin was made of pine because that's a wood soft enough to dissolve in the earth after a while. Now that wasn't so long ago, either. I can't think how we could have changed our ways so much, so *fast*."

"Well, Grandma's folks were immigrants and they had the Old World ways. How could we do that—like for Great-grandpa—if somebody died in the summer and people had to come from a long way for the funeral?"

She was finishing the carrots by then, setting them in salted, cold water off to one side and turning to the refrigerator to check for butter. All of this was automatic because she was thinking about what he'd said.

"Just *faster*, I suppose." She smiled slightly. "I don't think it's so important for far-off relatives to come and actually *look* at a dead person. It seems they should come to pray and most of all to take care of those who are left behind; they need a lot of holding up for a while."

"You wouldn't want people to look at you, Mama?"

She turned from the refrigerator with a solid pound of butter in her hand and paused for a long time.

"I wouldn't want *any* of it. I would want to be put in the earth like your father's grandpa. I would like to think that I might at least grow some flowers."

"I don't like it when you talk like that, Mama." Her serious tone was making him uneasy.

She grinned and reached over to mess his hair.

"Don't *you* worry about it, Toddy. Just go on and change your clothes. You've got to get started in the barn pretty soon. Now stop scowling like that. You can't do anything about it— nobody lives forever."

"All honor and glory are Yours, forever and ever, Amen."

The Great Amen was over, and the communion rite was about to begin. Todd kept watching the back of his father's head. That man had worn his mother to death, and then he wouldn't even listen to the way she wanted to be buried. Well, he was going to know it. The boy had it all worked out. Someday soon, when his father was beginning to calm down, he would take him aside and tell it all to him—the talk after Grandma Frederick's funeral and his mother's last words. He would make him understand that he'd violated the dying wish of his own wife. That was the little bomb the boy was silently preparing. A bomb for a bomb. Justice.

When everyone else rose to file past the casket to the communion rail, Todd remained kneeling stiffly. Let them think what they wanted. There were still two parts left to the ordeal, and he had to get himself mentally ready for them. The first was the graveside ceremony, where everyone crowded inside a canvas tent, shivering and trying to hide their hands inside their heavy coats. The coffin rested on a platform above the thick-sided cement vault. Father Schmidt, robed only as he had been in church, seemed anxious to finish this part quickly; his bare hands under the prayer folder were beginning to turn red.

"Let us pray. Almighty and merciful Father, You know the weakness of our nature; bow down Your ear in pity to Your servants. Lord, we beseech You, that while we lament the departure of our sister, Your servant, out of this life, we may bear in mind that we are most certainly to follow her. Grant that we may not languish in fruitless grief, nor sorrow as those who have no hope, but look meekly to you, the God of all consolation, through Christ our Lord, Amen."

And now everyone moved out of the tent, leaving the Fredericks huddled around the freezing flowers that covered the casket. Bob and Carol had to support the father, and Tony held the grandmother, more to warm her than to prevent her falling. Todd stood a little apart, wondering with numb detachment how they'd made that hole in the frozen ground.

Finally, the family turned to follow the throng back to the church hall. The coffin wouldn't be lowered in front of them; Mr. Shauer, who cared for the cemetery, would get some men to do that while everyone was inside. The only sounds were the brittle crunchings of boots and shoes in the snow.

Inside the hall, the warm air and the smells of food moved against cold faces like comforting hands. People began at once to snatch off steamed eyeglasses. Todd had steeled himself for this last part as for the worst: people all around saying stupid things, relatives he didn't even know forcing themselves upon his chosen silence, having to put food into his mouth as if this were just any other day. He was brought up short, though, by the actual display of food; he could not help but be impressed. Three long tables were covered completely with steaming pots of beans, German potato salad, and vegetables; whole hams and meat loaves were scattered among dozens of cold salads, rolls, and casseroles. At the end of the third table, cakes, pies, bars, and cookies were so crowded together that no part of the tablecloth showed through. No member of the family would ever know which woman had brought what food. It was another one of those things that just happened, one of the old ways these people had never unlearned.

People were beginning to line up awkwardly and silently at the plate-end of the long tables. Bob found the boy at the coat racks and took his arm.

"Come on, Todd." He was still whispering. "We're supposed to go through the line first."

The boy followed him and took a plate. His father was a few feet in front of him, and the boy found himself watching the man's hands as they reached for food: the long fingers were steady, no longer shaking. The boy reached for food too, without seeing what he took; he didn't like macaroni salad, but there it was on his plate next to a piece of ham. One table was for the family to sit at, and Todd waited deliberately for his father to sit down so that he could take a place at the opposite end, next to Bob's children. Just once, as he was sitting down, his father looked hard at him and frowned that little frown. Todd looked away first. With his back against the wall, he could watch all the other tables as they began to fill up with people.

He didn't try to eat. From almost complete silence, the noise level in the room was beginning to rise. First it was only the sounds of eating, silverware clanking, and chairs creaking. Then it was voices, people talking in normal tones to neighbors and to people they hadn't seen in some time. At the far end of the room, someone laughed out loud and no shocked silence fell. It happened again from somewhere nearer. People were talking louder now in order to hear each other over the noise.

Todd tried to resent the noise, to hate the people who laughed, but it wasn't working that way. It was almost as if the noise was trying to tell him something important, but he couldn't make it out.

"Can I go back for more, Uncle Todd?" Jason was three.

"*May* I, and I told you not to call me Uncle." He'd snapped the words before he remembered that he didn't want to talk. The little boy's lip was starting to tremble.

"Go on, Jason," Todd said in a softer voice. "Go feed your face."

The child slid down and hurried away, balancing his plate in front of him like a circus juggler.

People were beginning to get up and move around now, so Todd stood up from his untouched food and started for one of the entrances. He was anxious to think, but he was intercepted by some cousins, Tom and Arnie Frederick, who'd come down from Medford with their parents. They looked a little embarrassed, but they'd played with him in childhood and now felt obliged to say something.

"Well, Todd. It's been a while." Tom was older, so he began.

When Todd only nodded, Arnie tried.

"How's the old throwing arm? Hammern have a team that's worth anything this year?"

"Conference championship in November." Todd was startled by the sound of his own voice; he hadn't really intended to answer.

"Good enough," said Tom. Then, "Remember the old Frederick Follies?" This was a reference to the Halloween skits they'd put together when the cousins lived just down the road from each other.

"Yeah, I don't do that sorta stuff anymore."

"Yeah. Just kid stuff."

After an exchange of "See ya," the cousins walked away. Todd started to call after them, but it surprised him that he wanted to, so he stood there a little dazed and so deep in thought that he didn't see Mrs. Sensbauer come up to him. Betsy Sensbauer was his mother's close friend—they belonged to the same card club and had learned to knit together at a church-sponsored series of lessons. Betsy was a round, dark-haired woman who always made a striking contrast to his mother. Todd didn't look up when she greeted him, preparing himself for the expected sympathy that made him writhe inwardly with resentment.

"I didn't see you earlier, Todd, because I didn't go to the funeral parlor. I don't like that sort of thing."

His head snapped up, and his widened eyes met hers.

"Oh, you do look like your mother," she said softly. "I've been watching you across the room, and you are her image. Of course, you'll be tall like your father."

His eyes slid away from her. She'd been watching him. Somehow in his silent watchfulness, he'd felt invisible, an unobserved observer. She touched his face gently, and he looked back at her.

"Your mother was a fine person, you know. And such energy! I don't think I've ever met anyone who was so energetic. I used to tease her that no one had ever seen her sitting down."

She was looking at him very intently now, her brown eyes shining from the tears that stood in them.

"We should be glad, you know, that she didn't have to live as an invalid. I don't think she would have been able to bear that; it would have been a torture to her. I'm only saying this to you because you seem angry. I can understand that feeling a little, but you mustn't be angry with her for dying; she didn't mean to go away. She just couldn't help it, anymore than she could help being such a—such a driver."

The boy's mouth had dropped open. It had simply never occurred to him that his rage might be directed toward his mother; it seemed unimaginable that his feelings could be misinterpreted in that way. Nobody could be blamed for dying.

Mrs. Sensbauer pushed his hair to one side of his forehead and said, "Your family is back there, Todd. Maybe they're looking for you," and then she walked away.

The boy turned back toward the crowded room, unseeing, frowning in concentration. Was it possible that Betsy Sensbauer was right about his mother? Could it be that her constant motion, her endless working, her refusal to take care of herself were just part of the way she was, that she would have been that way—a driver—even if she hadn't married George Frederick? He shook his head sharply, causing his hair to fall down into his eyes; then he focused his attention on the other side of the room.

Clusters of people had gathered around each member of the family; everyone seemed to be talking normally. He saw Bob smiling at Aunt Esther, Elaine and Frank were sitting with Grandma, and Margaret had found a school friend who was also a cousin. Women were clearing the tables, and the clatter competed with the sounds of voices.

The largest group surrounded his father. It was not hard to find him, for he'd straightened up and was talking with his arms as usual. He *was* a tall man. It seemed almost as if the people around him were literally holding him up, buttressing him so he could stand straight like that.

The boy shivered suddenly and folded his thin arms across his chest; it was cold where he was standing, so close to the door. He'd taken a tentative step when Mrs. Pauly descended on him, talking on the run as usual.

"Run tell your father that Father Schmidt wants to talk to him. Something about a final prayer before people start drifting away."

He walked steadily across the room; it was a good reason, after all, wasn't it? By the time he had worked his way through the crowd, he noticed that a small woman still dressed in coat and gloves had joined the group around his father. She was talking animatedly, and his father had leaned forward so that his face almost touched the woman's absurdly bouffant hairdo. Todd moved in close enough to see that she was about sixty years old and that she was obviously upset.

Suddenly his father saw him and, reaching out quickly, caught Todd by the back of the neck to draw him in to face the woman.

"This is our baby—Todd," his father said, and the boy was so startled by the choice of words that he forgot to be resentful. "He's our serious one, a reader. You haven't seen him since he was seven. Todd, I'll bet you don't remember your Aunt Grace from California. She had some trouble coming up from O'Hare Field."

The woman was his mother's oldest sister.

"Why Todd, you *have* grown, haven't you? You're the *image* of your poor mother."

She kept talking as she stripped off her gloves. Todd stood there with his father's hand resting on the back of his neck, mesmerized. She didn't resemble his mother much, but his mother's voice was coming out of her mouth—the same intonation, gestures, inflections, the same tendency to emphasize words with her voice.

"Well, it was a *mad*house. The flight to Chicago was right on schedule and the motel was right there. But all this *snow* this morning! Nothing could get off the ground; they were definite about *that*. So I rented a car and here I'm late. I *knew* I'd be late."

So this was what it was going to be like. Down the long road of his life, he could expect to meet this at any moment—some reminder of his mother. A gesture, a voice, a turn of the head, a way of walking seen at a distance—all saying the same thing each time: "But remember, she is gone. She is not anywhere on this earth. You will never see her again." It might be some relative like this aunt or one of his sisters as they got older; it might be a stranger in a crowd or across a store counter.

The boy could feel his father's hand beginning to shake on the back of his neck; the trembling passed down through Todd's narrow shoulders and into his bones. He took a quick half-step backward so that his back and shoulders would support his father's forearm.

"Excuse me, Aunt Grace," he said briskly, interrupting her in mid-sentence. "The priest has to talk to Papa about a closing prayer."

His father cuffed him lightly on the back of the head and moved away without a word. Todd turned his back on the woman with his mother's voice and watched his father walk to meet the young priest. He noted with a sudden flash of panic that George Frederick was starting to look old.

Of course, he would never tell him now. What difference did it make? The only thing that mattered was that they would never see her again. Neither of them would ever see her again. He was beginning to cry now, but he didn't know it yet.

Changeling

(1979)

When he came through the door, she thought they'd made a mistake, brought the wrong prisoner, for this fat, balding man could not be her son. He was hunched inside the shapeless prison clothes, his chin against his collar. He glanced sideways at her.

"Hello, Ma," he said, and there was something in the voice she recognized, some reminder of all the times he'd been sorry for hurting her feelings, but was too proud to say so.

"Will?" she said. "Willy?"

He sat down before looking straight at her, sinking heavily onto the metal chair. His face was old, so much older than his thirty-seven years, and his eyes looked empty inside the puffy folds of skin. His hair, once so blond and fine, was now dull brown, hanging in long strings over his ears, but thin on the top of his head. On his forehead was a long scar that stood up like a ridge from his left eyebrow to what had once been his hairline.

"How was the bus, Ma?" he said, just like that, as if she had come across town instead of twelve hundred miles, as if it had been only yesterday since he'd seen her instead of fifteen years.

"It was a long way, Willy," she said. "And my legs ain't so good anymore. They swole up something awful. But I rested up overnight in the motel."

"How's things on the farm?"

"I don't live on the farm no more. Your letter finally come to me at the place where I'm staying now. I gave up the farm when your pa died."

He looked down at the table and shrugged the collar further up onto the back of his neck.

"Did you get a good price for it?" he asked.

"Ain't you gonna ask what your pa died of?" she said.

"No."

"I woulda let you know when it happened, but I didn't have no idea where to begin looking for you."

"I been lotsa places. No permanent address."

A silence fell. The old woman shivered and wrapped her arms around herself. It was not that the little visitors' room was cold; if anything, the air was overheated. It was just that everything was made of metal and tile, even the furniture; there was no wood, no fabric, nothing warm at all.

"Why didn't you write to me sooner," she said, "when all a' this started?"

"I didn't think it would come to this. I thought I'd get off. But them other assault charges really did me in."

"Other assault charges?"

"Yeah. A coupla fights. Only one conviction. Till this one, I mean. But the jury sorta took it into account." He spoke slowly, pausing between each of his sentences, as if he were not used to conversation.

"So now this manslaughter thing is gonna keep you here how long?" she asked.

"Five, six years. If I behave myself."

"Did you kill him, Willy?"

"He was shoving me around, Ma. Liquored up and cocky—"

"I don't want any a' the details. I just want to know if you killed this man."

"Yeah. I did."

"You didn't say that in the letter."

"I thought you wouldn't come."

"I'da come anyway, Willy. Now let's talk about something else."

"What's there to talk about?"

"I don't know. Home, maybe."

He grunted and looked away, but she went on, told him about the funerals, the births, the foreclosures, the storms—all the big things that had happened in Hammern since he headed south the day after his twenty-second birthday. Every now and then he would ask some question, and she would answer while he sat there, bent over toward her with his head nodding up and down. But they didn't talk about themselves.

When she was about to leave, he turned back to her from the metal door and said, without meeting her eyes, "Will you come again sometime?"

She thought it over for a minute.

"I don't know, Willy. It's a long way and the bus costs a lot of money. I ain't so young, either. I just don't know. We'll see."

As the Greyhound rolled north past the rich, sunny farmlands of Tennessee, the old woman leaned against the window and lifted her legs onto the cushion of the empty seat next to her. She tucked the faded cotton dress under her legs, adjusted her kerchief, and folded her hands onto the magazine in her lap. She couldn't remember any of the parts she'd tried to read. She stared unseeing across the aisle, past a large black woman who was feeding pieces of banana to her child.

The old woman was remembering. On the trip down, she'd remembered in all its frightening detail the day Willy had struck his father in the face with his fists and ran out of the house. Except for two letters and one postcard that came that same year, it was the last she'd heard of her son until the letter from prison. But now she was remembering an earlier day, a Saturday in winter the year Willy was eleven.

The day had begun badly, and Walter, the boy's father, was already in one of his black moods at breakfast. A cow was down. She'd fallen just outside the barn doors as Walter was trying to lead her to the truck. They'd had sickness with the cows all that winter, but Walter said the vet was too expensive and a quack at that, so the cows had to fight whatever it was by themselves. But this one hadn't got any better, so he was going to try to pass her off at the slaughterhouse. If that didn't work, he could just take the truck on over to the place that made dog food. But she'd fallen, and no amount of kicking and pulling could get her up again. So

Walter had had to call Pete Ashenbrenner and ask him to come over with his truck.

"Why isn't this slop hot?" Walter said, banging his spoon down into the oatmeal.

"I could heat it up for you," she said quietly. After fifteen years of marriage to this man, she knew better than to cross him when he was in this kind of mood.

"It don't matter," he said, shoving the bowl away from himself. "I ain't hungry anyway."

His brows were knit into a deep frown, but even when he wasn't angry, there were deep creases between his eyes, partly from squinting into the sun, partly from his being angry most of the time. He kept his brown hair cut very close to his square head and his ears stood out like flags. His mouth was wide and straight and looked like a line drawn across the bottom of his face.

He was staring across the table at Willy, and the mother felt the familiar sick feeling in her stomach. He was going to take it out on the boy, and there was nothing she could do to stop it.

"You feed them chickens?" Walter snarled.

The boy jerked upright. He'd been bent over his food, alternating scoops of oatmeal with bites of toast. He was large for his age, tall and just enough overweight for the kids at school to make fun of him.

"Sure," he said, his mouth still full. "Right after milking. You saw me go."

"Don't sass me! You eat like a pig, you know that? You're already almost as fat as the sow."

The boy reddened and lowered his head. He'd stopped chewing, so the toast just bulged inside his cheek.

"You get that from your mother's side," Walter said without even glancing at his wife. "Another thing you get from her is no brains. Ain't no idiots on the Reicher side of the family."

So they were both going to get it. She stood up and began to stack her own dishes.

"This meal ain't finished yet," he said in the controlled tone she'd learned to fear. When he talked in that tone, pretending to be calm like that, it meant that the next thing was the hitting, unless she could get him onto something else.

She sat back down quickly, not looking at him.

"Let me bring you some more coffee," she said.

"You do that," he said. "And make sure it's hot."

She brought the coffee from the stove, half-running because she knew any sign of slowness would give him an excuse to be even more angry.

"You don't have to fly around like you was on a broomstick," he said, but his voice had gone back to the shouting, which was safer.

Willy had begun to chew again, and this drew Walter's attention.

"You don't forget your other chores this morning," he said. "I got to go to the mill to get some oats ground, so you got the milk machines to do by yourself."

Willy nodded and swallowed.

"And you watch for Ashenbrenner. I got to pay good money to have him winch that damn cow up off the driveway." His brows closed together again. "You hear me?" he said and reached across the table to cuff the boy on the side of the head.

Without even looking up, Willy dodged away so that the blow just grazed his ear. He'd got used to being hit, his mother thought, had learned how to duck when he was just a little boy. It was why she never hit him herself.

"I got a big load on my back," Walter said, beginning a familiar speech. "And I get precious little help. Other men got lots of sons, but I got only one worthless bull calf like you. That's thanks to your ma, too."

She was used to this. The operation after Willy was born had meant she could never have any more children, and that too had become a reason for Walter to yell at her, even to hit her sometimes when he was feeling especially angry.

"If that damn Pete Ashenbrenner can't come right away when

116   Winter Roads, Summer Fields

I call him, he can just wait for his money too," Walter said, standing up. "I'm getting the oats in the truck, so you two can get to work now."

He struggled into his plaid wool jacket, punching his arms into the sleeves, and pulled on his blackened work gloves. Then he walked out the back door without another word.

Willy went back to his oatmeal without looking at his mother. She thought as she began clearing dishes that she rarely saw her son's eyes anymore. They had once been a clear, bright blue like a June sky, but they'd become paler lately, almost the color of the ice on the pond. And they were seldom still, but moved back and forth even when his face was lifted to the person talking to him.

When she came back from the cupboard after rinsing the coffee cups, she found Willy getting into his jacket. He knew it was important for his father to see him getting a start on cleaning the milk machines before the truck left for town. She walked up behind him and put her hand on his shoulder. He jerked away, throwing his upper body out of her reach, and then he stomped out of the house, making a lot of noise with the storm door.

So he was blaming her, she thought. She'd noticed that more and more often lately, especially this last year. It was as if he expected her to protect him, to get between him and his father, and he was angry with her when she didn't. He couldn't see that she was quiet for a reason, that it would only make things worse if she tried to stick up for him. Whenever Walter thought somebody was against him, was sassing him, he got meaner. And Willy couldn't see the way she sometimes got around Walter, got him to do a few things that Willy wanted, because that was done in such a quiet way, had to be done so roundabout.

Of course, Willy was still feeling sore about the 4-H. In September, he'd come home from school full of talk about joining the 4-H. His teacher had explained the club to them and talked about projects and trips for the year. Some of the kids had signed up right away, without even asking their parents, Willy said. Lloyd Bouduin was going to raise a calf of his own for the county fair next year, and one of the field trips was going to be to the railroad museum.

"So can't I join, Mama, can't I?" Willy pleaded.

It was one of those afternoons she enjoyed. Walter was out in the fields finishing up the corn and so was not in the house waiting for Willy to come from school; on such rare days, she had time to talk to the boy before he started his chores.

"You know you have to ask your pa," she'd said, kneading a large lump of dough, her arms and apron front covered with flour.

"He'll say no," Willy said, his eager face clouding up. "You know he doesn't let me do anything I want to do. You can tell the teacher it's all right for me to be in the club."

"I can't do no such thing, Willy, and you know it. He'd never let up on us for a year if we went behind his back like that. And he'd take you right back out of the thing anyway."

"I really wanna be in the 4-H, Ma."

She stopped punching the dough for a moment and looked at his face. He almost never asked for anything anymore, never mentioned movies that other kids got to see, sometimes three or four times, but he seemed to really care a lot about this 4-H thing.

"I'll try to talk to him," she finally said. "Now remember, I ain't promising nothing, cuz you know as well as I do how your pa can be, but I'm gonna try."

He jumped forward to hug her, paying no attention to the dough on her hands and the flour on her clothes. She was taken by surprise—he didn't often hug her anymore—and almost fell, but he was already a big boy and steadied her, laughing a little at the surprised look on her face.

She'd waited until she thought Walter was in a good mood, the next evening when the corn was all in the silo and after he'd seemed to enjoy the spareribs at supper. Willy was upstairs doing his homework, and the ball game hadn't started yet on the radio. But she'd miscalculated after all.

"What the hell does he need to be in the 4-H for?" he snapped as soon as she mentioned it.

Winter Roads, Summer Fields

"The 4-H teaches good things," she answered. "He can get into projects that can even make money in the long run."

"Not unless I lay out good money first, I can tell you. George Pankratz had to pay for feeding and pampering his boy's pig just so's it could get some cheap ribbon at the fair. There ain't nothing you can tell me about that stuff that I don't already know."

"He could learn stuff about farming."

"You trying to say I don't know enough about farming to teach him what he needs to know?" And his eyes narrowed.

"No, no. Just different stuff." She was getting desperate and so changed the subject. "He could make some new friends."

"He got all the friends he needs."

"He don't have no friends at all, Walter," she said, very quietly.

"Well, that's his own damn fault! He's so stupid and sulky nobody can take to him."

"A boy his age should have friends, and this here's a chance."

"He don't need friends." Walter was beginning to get that wild look that came on whenever he felt anyone was against him, or maybe criticizing him. "He got his work to do at home, and he can't go traipsing off to clubs to fool around with spoiled, snobby kids. I need him on the place. It might be different if I had four sons like George Pankratz got." And then he began the familiar speech that blamed her for almost every piece of bad luck in their lives, so she knew it was no use; she'd lost.

The next morning, before Willy left to wait for the school bus, she said simply to him, "He said no."

"You didn't ask him right," Willy had cried. "You didn't try," and he stamped out of the house just the way he'd done this cold winter morning four months later. She guessed he had to have somebody to blame, and he couldn't sass his father, couldn't say much to him at all.

About nine-thirty, she decided to carry out the slop pail for the pigs. She'd been watching out the west window for Pete Ashenbrenner's truck, hoping to make only one trip out into the

Winter Roads, Summer Fields

windy, ice-slicked yard, but she didn't feel she could get at her other work until the bucket of peels and table scraps was out of the kitchen. So she pulled on her old tweed coat, wrapped a long woolen scarf around her head and lower face, and carried the pail outside.

The two barn buildings formed a backwards "L" shape, with the pig barn as the longer arm; from the back door of the house, she had to walk around that building towards its west-side door before she could see the dairy barn and the doors where Walter had tried to lead out the sick cow. The cow was still lying there where she'd fallen. The wind was whipping the snow up off the large banks near the place where the two buildings met, blowing the stinging snow right into the woman's face, so at first she didn't notice Willy.

But then he moved, and she could see his dark jacket against the white of the Holstein's bony shoulder. Willy was kneeling next to the cow's head with his back to his mother, so crouched over that she couldn't see his head. She stopped where she was, the pail pulling at the end of her arm.

Willy leaned over the cow's head as if he were talking to it. Then, suddenly, the sick animal tried to get up, flinging her legs outward the way downed cows do when they're on their sides, trying to roll over onto her knees. But she was too weak; she rolled back over again, her head lifting and then falling down. Again Willy bent over and, after a minute or two, the cow tried again to rise, but this time her effort was even weaker. She made a faint moaning sound that could just be heard above the wind.

The mother's heart squeezed in her breast. Her son was trying to help the poor beast, trying to get her up so that she wouldn't have to be dragged by a winch up the ramp to Ashenbrenner's truck. Maybe he thought that the cow might still fetch a price at the slaughterhouse if she could be got to walk into the truck. The mother hadn't known that Willy talked to the farm animals—he had no pets—but then she didn't often go into the dairy barn anymore. She set the pail down and walked slowly toward Willy, her footsteps making almost no sound in the snow, her other movements covered by the noise of the wind. She wanted to hear what Willy was saying.

She was within four feet of him when she heard the unmistakable sound of a match being struck against the rough side of a box.

"Willy?" she said, puzzled.

He whirled around, his head jerking up the way it did when his father spoke to him unexpectedly. Almost before he saw his mother, his face looked guilty as well as surprised.

She stood there looking down at the scene which seemed to leap into sharp focus out of the blur of swirling snow. Even after all these years, she could still see it clearly in all its details: Willy kneeling there, looking down now, smoke drifting away from the wind-snuffed match in his hand; the gravel showing gray all around the cow where the heat of her body had melted the snow; the big head lolling on its left side with stones pressing into the soft muzzle; the fresh burn marks on the inside of the ear and all around the staring, white-rimmed eye.

It was perhaps twenty seconds before the mother raised her arm and brought the back of her hand down across Willy's face. He tipped over sideways into the snow and then sprang back up into a crouch. At first his face looked only surprised, his mouth open, his hand, still holding the match, lifted to his cheek. Then he looked sideways up at her, his eyes narrowing into hatred.

She turned and ran back to the house, past the slop pail still steaming in the snow. All the rest of the morning, she sat at the kitchen table in her coat and scarf. She didn't go outside when she heard Ashenbrenner's truck; she didn't even go to the window. She just sat there wondering when and how it had happened. When had somebody stolen away her beautiful baby with the angel hair and eyes like a summer sky, and left in his place this big, ugly, mean-eyed boy?

Winter Roads

(1983)

It was already snowing when they got up the morning after Thanksgiving. Sharon leaned against the windowsill and watched the fine snow driving across the road, straight from the north. Steam rising from her coffee cup soon clouded the window and she turned away.

"Well, it looks like we're going to keep you here longer than you planned," her father said from his place at the dining room table. He too was nursing a cup of coffee. Sharon had sent him the robe the previous Christmas, but it looked suspiciously new, as if he'd taken it out of the box only recently.

"You don't think it's going to stop?" she said.

"Radio says it's a real blizzard. Probably eight or ten inches by tomorrow and lots of blowing."

"It's too early for this, isn't it?" she said impatiently.

He chuckled a little.

"You've been living in the Southland too long. Late November may be fall down there, but it's winter up here."

"Yes, I remember. And late August is already fall."

Of course she remembered; the early blizzards, the late blizzards, the cold spells when the temperature never rose above zero for ten days at a time. Her father and uncles had names for the big storms—the May Blizzard of '39, the Hunters' Blizzard of '63—and they spoke the names with the same combination of awe and pride that veterans use to talk of long-ago battles.

Sharon sighed and sank down onto a chair next to her father.

"It's just that I'm worried about catching our plane," she said.

"Well it could be all over by Sunday morning, of course. But if it isn't, there's just nothing we can do about it anyway. You'll have to call your boss and fill him in on northern winters."

"Well, I don't suppose Lisa will mind missing another day or two of school."

"I'm just selfish enough to be glad," he said. "We got you two here at last, and we want to hang onto you as long as we can."

She smiled and reached out to cover his hand with her own. He took a sip of coffee and glanced at the closed door to his left.

"I hope Mom sleeps another hour or two," she said, following his thought. "Yesterday must have been a strain for her, even if she didn't complain."

"Well, the doctor says she should do what she always does but just a lot slower, and she needs to rest. The medicine helps that because it slows her heart and lowers her blood pressure."

"Has she had any pains since she started on this medicine?" Sharon asked, relieved to have this opportunity to talk about it with him; since their arrival on Wednesday evening, the conversation had veered away from specifics.

"A few, but not bad ones, and she has the nitroglycerin for that."

"Have the doctors really ruled out surgery?"

"They don't think it's necessary. A few years ago, Doc Olson says, everybody was doing bypass surgery like it was a tonsillectomy, but they aren't so eager anymore. They think they can control the angina with medication."

"They think. But they're not sure."

"Well, sweetie, very little in this life is certain."

She couldn't remember the last time he'd called her "sweetie," and it brought tears to her eyes. He cleared his throat and stood up, slowly, with his left hand pushing down on the table for support. Watching his movements, she felt a stab of fear, and it must have shown on her face, because he chuckled again and said, "Just the arthritis. It acts up in the morning. Too many years of plowing on an open tractor, I guess," and he went back into the kitchen for more coffee.

Sharon found herself remembering the first time it had occurred to her that her father was not immortal. It was perhaps fifteen years ago in this very room, when she was in college and home for Christmas vacation. Her father was changing a light bulb in the hallway, standing on a chair facing her with his arms lifted above his head, intent on the task for which his hands seemed too clumsy. He'd had his upper teeth pulled that fall and was still having a hard time adjusting to his dentures; despite regular nagging from his wife he kept taking them out, and he wasn't wearing them that afternoon. Sharon had looked up from her book just as the bulb lit up flooding her father's face with harsh light. At that angle, without his teeth, he looked like a cadaver, the cords under his chin stretched and obvious as those uncovered by an instructor's scalpel.

He'd jumped down from the chair, transformed into her robust father again, but the image had stayed somewhere in the back of her mind, like a face in a nightmare, ready to spring into consciousness at odd times when her guard was down. Now that she lived so far away and saw her parents so seldom, the signs of their aging came as even greater shocks to her, for she'd kept them in her mind as healthy people in their early fifties. When her father had called her in September to tell her about her mother's angina, she'd cried for hours after hanging up the phone.

"It's snowing!" Lisa burst into the dining room with this announcement, her short hair awry from sleep, her eyes dancing with excitement.

"Shhh. You'll wake Grandma," Sharon said.

"Okay, okay. But isn't it great? Grandpa, it's snowing. Can we borrow Mr. Grassel's snowmobile?"

"Maybe later today, after there's more snow on the ground," he said, laughing at the way she bounced when she talked. "Let's see what we can find for your breakfast. Probably not turkey, huh?"

Watching them rummaging in the cupboards, Sharon smiled at the fact that her father had lived most of his life in this house without ever seeming to learn where things were kept. Lisa's dark head bobbed next to his shoulders as he bent to look into the bread box. It would make a wonderful photograph, Sharon thought, a lasting image of this mutual adoration society. Lisa had lived all of her nine years in Atlanta, and she didn't see her grandparents often, but the farm lived in her imagination like some fairyland, and its undisputed monarchs were Grandpa and Grandma. They were the dispensers of magic: baby calves, hayrides, fascinating machines, woods alive with wild rabbits and field mice.

And, Sharon thought, it was only natural that Lisa would be thrilled with the snow; she seldom saw it at home, and she wasn't responsible for moving it out of the way or for getting through it to some necessary destination. To her, the snow was both delightful for its own sake and precious because it suspended time, sided with play, held off the adult world. Sharon remembered her own secret joy as a child watching the roads filling up with snow. Buses couldn't come, parents couldn't go into town, sometimes even the mailman couldn't bring the newspaper and bills. Then she could bundle up and walk across the road to her cousins' farm, sinking in snow drifts up to her hips. It was always a disappointment when the snowplow came because it meant that life would have to become ordinary again.

"What do you suppose they're doing over there?" Sharon's mother spoke from the bedroom doorway. Sharon jumped a little because she hadn't heard the door open.

"Burning toast, I think," she said, getting up to greet her mother. "What are you doing up?"

"Oh, you know I never could sleep late. Besides you don't need so much sleep when you get old."

"Let me get you some coffee."

"No, I have to drink decaffeinated now," she said, making a face. "I'll make myself a cup in a little while. Let's just sit down and visit."

This was a new development too. In the past, Sharon thought, her mother would have rushed into the kitchen to take over. Now she simply walked to a chair and sat down, and Sharon was struck by how small she looked inside the floor-length robe; she carried herself carefully, her shoulders hunched forward as she walked, as if she were trying to protect her chest from some half-expected blow.

"I think Lisa is having a good time, don't you?" she said.

"Of course," Sharon answered. "She loves it here, and she should, the way you and Dad spoil her."

"I'm glad to see she's not much changed."

"You mean since the divorce? It's all right to say it out loud, Mom, really it is. Yes, Lisa is doing pretty well. She keeps her feelings a little more to herself than she used to, and she worries more."

"Worries?"

"About things in general. About me in particular. Lectures me on safe driving every time I leave the house."

"Well, she's probably had enough of losing people for a while."

"She sees him every other weekend, Mom."

"But it's not the same."

"No," Sharon said, her voice tightening. "It's not the same. But we're going to be all right."

The old irritations, she found, were closer to the surface than she'd imagined. Her mother's assumptions about family life, about religion, about women "working," all projected with the certainty that her daughter must assent, must conform—all of the old patterns still had the power to arouse Sharon's defiance.

"A child should have two parents." Her mother actually said the predictable thing. "And you should have more children, Sharon. Lisa shouldn't have to grow up alone."

"You mean the way I did?" Sharon said before she could stop herself. Instantly she felt her stomach twist with fear. Her mother must not be upset or excited, the doctor had said. And so here was another of the curses of aging—they couldn't even have a good fight anymore.

But her mother didn't fire up as she once would have; she looked away and said softly, "You weren't alone. You had Johnny until you were eight, and you would've had more brothers and sisters if I hadn't lost the other ovary after you were born."

"I know, Mother," Sharon sighed. "I'm sorry."

Her father came from the kitchen carrying a glass of milk and several bottles of pills.

"Take your medication now, Laura," he said. "And in a few minutes your granddaughter and I will bring your breakfast. It's a surprise." He grinned and winked at them.

The women watched him pad back into the kitchen, and then Laura began to shake tablets into her left hand.

"How is Dad doing since he sold the land to Grassel?" Sharon asked, grateful for a chance to change the subject. "Is he really adjusting to his retirement?"

"Well, retirement isn't always an easy change," her mother said, setting down the glass. "I think it may be even harder for farmers. I still catch him watching the skies sometimes. But he's got lots of projects going right now, and he sometimes helps out the Grassel boys. Of course, since September he's been pretty much underfoot. He's afraid to leave me alone."

"Well, you can't blame him, can you?"

"I guess not. I don't really mind, you know."

"I know, Mom."

By noon the sky was thick with snow, big flakes that stuck to the side of the machine shed and brought the horizon very close to the house. Lisa had already been outside once and had come back in, soaking wet and pink-cheeked. When Sharon went upstairs to make beds, she could hear the wind moaning under the eaves, a sound that had so frightened her as a child that she'd learned to fall asleep with her pillow firmly wrapped around her head.

The wind had been howling like that the night Johnny was killed. Even now, she always thought the word "killed" about him, never "died." It was as if the violence, the suddenness of his death had never completely faded for her since that night when his car had skidded off an ice-slicked road and into a tree. So she'd grown up thinking of death as something that pounced out of nowhere, an efficient predator that granted its victims the mercy of oblivion without any mounting terror ahead of time. She knew that her father had seen death in the war in France, but he seldom spoke of it, so the very mystery of those deaths made them seem remote, even a little romantic.

Only recently had she begun to see death as something that approached gradually, almost casually coming closer and closer while she watched it all the time, fighting it away with rationalizations. Uncle Hank had died of cancer at fifty, but that was a fluke, and besides, he wasn't very close to her, really. Then Grandma Tomchek, but she was old; her husband's father, but he was, after all, not her own father. One person at a time, death marched closer until it began to look familiar, less horrible but also less arbitrary, more inevitable; it no longer seemed possible, as it had when she was a child, that death might miss her, pass her by.

When Sharon came back down into the dining room, she found her mother sitting on the edge of a chair, so hunched forward that her forehead almost touched the polished surface of the table.

"What's wrong, Mom?" Panic almost closed Sharon's throat so that she gasped rather than spoke the question.

"I don't feel so good." Her voice sounded very small.

Sharon squatted beside her and looked into her face, which was ashen and sagged forward as if all the muscles had suddenly let loose from their moorings. For some reason, Sharon was reluctant to touch her.

"*How* do you feel bad? Are you in pain?"

"No. I just feel so weak and dizzy that I can't even sit up. And I feel like I might throw up."

Sharon took hold of her mother's arms and almost let go from the shock. The arms were cold and damp.

"Dad?" Sharon called, sharp and urgent.

Her father came at once from the living room where he and Lisa had been playing checkers.

"What's the matter, Laura?" he said when he saw them crouched together.

"I don't know." Her voice was even fainter.

"She feels weak and nauseated, but she doesn't have any pain," Sharon said quickly, alarmed by the sudden pallor in her father's face.

He moved surprisingly quickly, pulling another chair next to his wife and folding her against his body as he sat down.

"Should I get your nitroglycerin?" he said.

She shook her head "no."

"Just in case?" He was whispering.

"No pain," she said. Her breathing was fast and shallow.

"I think she should go to the hospital, Dad," Sharon said.

He nodded, his chin grazing his wife's hair. "Call the Rescue Squad."

Sharon turned to the wall phone behind her, groping for the shelf where the phone book was kept. Lisa had come into the room but stood with her back against the door frame, her eyes large and moist.

"Inside the cover," Sharon heard her father say from behind her.

When she opened the book, she found the number at once. The words "Rescue Squad" were written in her mother's neat, rounded handwriting; next to the number was another number and the word "Priest."

"We need the Rescue Unit at George Tomchek's farm," Sharon said hurriedly into the phone. "Seidl's Road, fire number 406. My mother's had some kind of attack."

"We'll be right there," a familiar voice responded.

Sharon turned from the phone and put her arm around Lisa's rigid shoulders. Her father rocked her mother gently back and forth.

"Would you like to lay down, honey?" he asked softly.

"No," she whispered. "I feel like I'm going to throw up."

"I'll get the scrub pail, Dad," Sharon said. "She shouldn't try to walk."

In the chilly back entrance, she found the plastic pail exactly where her mother had always kept it. Inside again, she tried as quietly and unobtrusively as possible to place the pail next to her mother's feet, for she knew this woman's fastidiousness and was aware that, even under these circumstances, her mother would be embarrassed to throw up in front of people.

Her father held and rocked her mother, who was huddled against his chest. This was the same scene she'd found years ago when the sheriff had pounded on the door, handed the soaking wallet to her father, and announced Johnny's death. She'd heard the pounding, heard the first terrible wail when her mother was told, and had wrapped the pillow around her head, staring into the dark. Only when the sheriff's car had left the driveway did she creep down the stairs to find her parents like this. Then, as now, she felt the privacy of their experience, felt outside it, helpless.

"Get the afghan from the living room," Sharon said to Lisa.

The child responded instantly. Sharon and her father wrapped the bright afghan around her mother's shoulders, piling the ends into her lap. He looked up once at Sharon, his eyes bewildered and swimming in tears. She folded her arms and walked quickly to the window. Only now, looking out into the storm, did it occur to her to worry about whether the Rescue Squad would have trouble getting to them. She began to feel the prickly sensation of panic at the back of her scalp. The village of Hammern had inaugurated the new service only two years before, and the Squad was made up of volunteers summoned by beepers whenever a call came in. How efficient could they be?

But Sharon had walked into the living room to look out the east windows only three times when she saw the flashing lights. Incredibly, the ambulance had arrived just fifteen minutes after Sharon's call, and the village was three miles away. It crossed Sharon's mind that an emergency call in Atlanta would probably not produce results nearly this fast.

Winter Roads

She held the door open for them, and they swept past her into the dining room, carrying cases and an oxygen tank. Sharon was surprised to see that she recognized one of them as a high school classmate.

"Donna Merens," she said.

"Donna Arendt now," the other woman replied, smiling a little as she took out the blood pressure sleeve. The sound of the separating velcro exploded like a gunshot into the silence. A tall young woman stood on the other side of the patient, taking her pulse and then making notations on a clipboard. Donna pumped up the sleeve once, listening with the stethoscope and watching the dial. The hissing of the escaping air was the only sound in the room. She pumped it up again and then raised her eyes to the young woman with the clipboard. Sharon saw the puzzled little frown.

"We'll try the other arm," Donna said.

When she'd made two more efforts on the other arm, she whispered some numbers to the young woman, who silently wrote them down.

"What is it?" Sharon whispered as Donna stood up.

"Low. Very low," she answered. "Close to shock."

"Would the oxygen help?" Sharon's father asked. Two rumpled, unshaven men stood by, one on either side of the tank.

"I don't think so," Donna said. "In fact, I think she's been hyperventilating: too much oxygen." She turned to the two men and added, "Get the stretcher. She belongs in the hospital."

Sharon had forgotten how direct and no-nonsense Donna Merens could be.

"Is it her heart?" Sharon's father asked the question they had been avoiding.

"Can't tell," Donna said, quickly packing up her equipment. "We'll keep her stable and get her to people who will be able to tell us more."

"Am I going to the hospital?" Sharon's mother said, raising

her head slightly. It was as if they'd all forgotten that she was conscious.

"Yes, darling, that's best," her husband said, bending over her again.

"Thank you for getting here so fast," Sharon said to Donna, feeling that rush of gratitude often directed to those who lift, however little, the burdens of terror and responsibility.

"We've got the drill down pretty good," Donna smiled. "And there's no traffic out here to worry about."

In just a few minutes, the volunteers had moved Sharon's mother onto the wheeled stretcher, covered her with a blanket, and strapped her down. Sharon realized for the first time that she also knew one of the men; the taller and younger one was Todd Frederick, whom she remembered as a skinny kid—surely that was just yesterday, wasn't it, when Todd Frederick was a child? The tall young woman wrapped a white towel over the patient's head, draping the ends around her face.

"Here's Hal," Todd said, glancing at the south window.

"Hal?" Sharon said, following his gaze.

"Hal Timmons. Drives a county snowplow. The radio says the roads are worse to the west, and I figured we might need an escort."

And, sure enough, a huge yellow snowplow was waiting at the end of the driveway, its cab-top lights going around and around.

"Can I ride in the ambulance?" Sharon's father said.

"Sure," the other man said. "You can ride up front with me."

"I'll follow in your car, Dad," Sharon said.

Everyone turned to look at her.

"Don't you think it would be better for you to just stay here?" her father said. He looked over at Lisa. "I'll check in with you just as soon as we know anything. The car will just get snowed in at the hospital."

Now Sharon's mother opened her eyes. "You'd better stay home to answer the phone," she said. "Everybody from here to

Seidl's Corner must have seen the ambulance. They'll be calling up and down to see what's the matter."

Sharon looked down at her mother's face. Now that she was lying on her back, the flesh had fallen back into place and she looked surprisingly young. She was smiling.

"You're incorrigible, Mom. You really are."

They were moving the stretcher now, and Sharon ran ahead to hold the door. As her mother passed her, Sharon reached out to touch her cheek. When the men paused at the steps, her mother looked past Sharon into the snow.

"Funny," she said softly. "Just yesterday, the lawn was all green."

Sharon and Lisa stood in the driving snow and watched the ambulance pull out behind the plow; they watched, shivering, until they could no longer see the taillights of the ambulance.

Inside again, Lisa spoke for the first time.

"Do you think they'll get to the hospital all right?"

Sharon looked at the pale, tight little face. So young, she thought, to hold so much inside.

"Yes, sweetie, don't worry," she said. "When people live so much of the time with winter, they learn how to handle it. This looks bad to you, but it's really nothing much to them."

Sharon picked up the afghan from the floor and wrapped it around Lisa. They sat at the table.

"The winter I was eleven," Sharon said, "I had an appointment to have my eyes checked at a place close to the hospital where Grandma is going. We had tons of snow that winter, just tons. And the day before my appointment, we had another big blizzard."

"Bigger than this?"

"Bigger than this. The next morning, the snowplow came through just once, opening a lane right down the middle of the road. By noon, the sun was shining like crazy, and Grandma decided we should go to the eye doctor after all. You know how she hates to break appointments or be late for anything."

"Like going to church so early?"

"Yes, like that. So we all three got in the car and started off. The cleared part of the road was just wide enough for the car, and the snow banks on both sides were so high that they went over the car in most places. It was like driving in a tunnel. If we'd got stuck, we couldn't have opened the doors. But we went barreling along for the first couple of miles."

"Grandpa doesn't drive fast."

"You're right. I just meant that we went along easily without seeing anybody else. But halfway between Drossart's Road and Highway P we could see another car coming toward us. Well, there was no way for the two cars to pass each other, so we just came to a stop, and he came to a stop. Grandpa recognized him—somebody from the village."

"Grandpa knows everybody."

"It seems that way, doesn't it? Well, we just sat there for a minute, him staring at Grandpa and Grandpa staring at him; nobody opened a window to talk. Then the other man put his car in reverse and backed all the way to Highway P. We went forward after him. At the highway, he backed to the south as we turned north. We waved at each other. It was such a bright, sunny day, so still after the storm, and the snow sparkled like diamonds."

"It sounds like fun."

"It was. It was like an adventure."

"Do you think it was fun for Grandma and Grandpa?"

"Yes, I think so. At first, Grandma was embarrassed about making the other man back up, but Grandpa said *he* probably didn't have an appointment to get to in twenty minutes. After a while, Grandma got the giggles because the man *did* look funny with his head turned around and his car weaving back and forth."

Lisa stopped shivering at last. After a pause, she said, "Do you think it makes Grandma and Grandpa feel sad that they don't have any boys in the family?"

"What made you think of such a thing?" Sharon asked, startled.

"I don't know." Lisa shrugged under the afghan. "They have only us, and we don't even have the same name as them. Daddy says people want their names to go on—you know, after them."

Sharon put her arm across Lisa's shoulders and gave her a little squeeze.

"I honestly think Grandma and Grandpa don't give that a thought. We're their family no matter what our name is, and they're just crazy about us. You know that. They're so proud of you."

Lisa smiled, a brave little smile that didn't erase the fear in her eyes. For just a second, Sharon saw, superimposed over her daughter's face, the image of her mother's face on the stretcher, smooth and young again, almost as pale as the towel that surrounded it, smiling up at her, trying to deny the panic that clouded her eyes. Lisa's eyes were exactly the same color as her grandmother's.

At two o'clock, Sharon's father called to say that her mother was feeling a little better, but the doctors still hadn't made a diagnosis. The EKG didn't suggest that she'd had a heart attack, but her heart rate was very slow and her blood pressure was low. Somewhat encouraged, Sharon and Lisa managed to prepare a little lunch, but they ate in silence, listening to the wind howling across the flat farmlands outside.

It was not until after four that the phone rang again.

"It was the medicine!" Sharon's father sounded triumphant. "Her heart medicine that she takes every morning just built up until it was doing its job better than it should. The doctors say it works different for different people. Some people build up a resistance to the stuff and have to take more, but others sort of accumulate it in their tissues and have to reduce the dose. That's your mother all over, you know: always saving things up."

And he laughed so loud that Sharon had to take the receiver away from her ear for a minute.

"Can she come home right away?"

"Not until tomorrow, and then only if her heart rate is back up to sixty. I'm just going to bunk in here tonight. No sense trying to go anywhere in this storm anyway."

"We can come get you both tomorrow."

"You wait until I call. And you don't try it until this blow is all done and the roads are clear, either. We're all safe and sound where we are."

"Okay, Dad. When the roads are clear."

"Been listening to the radio in here, and the weatherman says clear and sunny by tomorrow morning. Guess you'll make your plane on Sunday."

"No. I'm going to call my boss tonight to tell him we're staying a few more days."

"Good. Your mother will be glad."

"Give her our love, Dad. And you have a good night's sleep."

Not until she'd hung up the phone did Sharon realize that tears had been running down her face all the while she'd been talking to her father. Now Lisa finally broke down too, sobbing against her mother's shoulder. Sharon pulled her onto her lap and sat there next to the window, rocking the child back and forth.

"It's all right, baby. Grandma just took too much medicine, and it made her sick for a little while. She's better now, and tomorrow she'll be better still. She's all right. Grandma's all right."

In her mind, she couldn't stop the unspoken rest of the sentence from echoing over and over: "This time. This time." Past Lisa's head, she stared out the window and across the lawn to where the snowdrifts were reaching out their tapering fingers, closing slowly but inexorably over the road.

Last Harvest

(1985)

Dust engulfed the little car within a quarter-mile after it had turned off the county highway onto a narrow gravel road.

"Damn!" Fran thought. "I always forget. A hell of a lot of good it did me to have this car washed before I left."

She slowed the car to a crawl, and the grinding of the gravel under the tires diminished to a low growl. As the solid-state radio became audible, a voice was proclaiming Coke as "the real thing." Outside the windows, the stripped fields drifted away, the tinted glass making the oat stubble look greenish brown in the late August sunshine. A sagging wreck of a house floated into view outside the passenger window. The doors were boarded up, and two front windows, their glass long shattered, turned a baleful, resigned stare at the passing car. Among the waist-high weeds in the lawn, two apple trees drooped under the weight of the fruit no one picked anymore. Once Fran had played here, soaring skyward on the unpainted board swing which still hung from one of the trees and squealing in mock terror as her godfather postponed his afternoon chores to push her, for hours it seemed, on the hot summer days. But like his house, he too was dead now, and her father's brother owned the land.

"It's such an eyesore," she thought irritably, fighting the memories as the house disappeared behind the car. "Uncle Peter should just tear it down."

A stand of corn on the neighboring farm, her cousins', seemed forest-high surrounded by the flattened fields, yet it in turn was dwarfed by a huge, shapeless machine, gleaming red and bristling with power even in its repose.

"*Their* latest status symbol," she thought, catching sight of herself in the rearview mirror. At thirty-five, she was already beginning to exhibit the characteristic family features, the heavy lower face, the thick body bequeathed by generations of peasant farmers. In the mirror, the thin vertical line between her eyebrows was exaggerated by her carefully acquired summer tan.

A sudden flash of irritation turned into annoyance at having to make this trip the very day she was expecting delivery of the new love seat that would put the finishing touch on her living room. How she loved the peace and order of her suburban apartment, furnished piece by piece over the past five years; the tasteful study with bright rows of books forming a background for her oak desk; the elegant little dinner parties for friends whose shoptalk was never boring because their shop—the world of books and theater—was her shop too.

But it was just like Henry to do this, self-importantly calling a family meeting, making an imminent crisis out of a question whose answer was self-evident and had been for three years. Sooner or later, the farm would have to go and everyone knew it; she'd told him so on the phone, but he'd insisted that they had to gather in force and in person or Papa would certainly "blow" the best chance of his life. She'd stalled, but he knew summer session was over and that the repairs on I-90 were finished at last. In the end, she just ran out of excuses. So four and a half-hours ago, she'd hung a blouse and denim skirt in the back of the car and started east.

Except for the obligatory appearances at Christmas and Easter, Fran had gotten out of the habit of going to the farm. For the most part her work was accepted as a valid excuse for long absences. Summers were harder until she discovered the trick of traveling. She could almost see her mother's face, soft and mildly hurt, explaining to puzzled relatives, "Oh, Fran spends most of the time traveling with friends." "Friends" was actually Julia Peterson, a fortyish divorcée whose thin energy and brittle worldliness bustled Fran through Italian museums, German libraries, and Mexican markets.

To Julia and other colleagues, Fran would always say, "I have so little in common with my family anymore; we haven't more than three days worth of things to say to each other at any one time."

She always said that because she couldn't tell them the real reason she avoided the farm. It was the memories. Whenever she was there, memories came upon her like blows struck when she wasn't looking. Anything could trigger them—a scene, a word, a gesture—and she was helpless to stop them. They had none of the pleasant sadness of nostalgia about them, but seared her like physical pain. Her present life and her work were steady and soothing. "Happiness" was a word she'd rejected as "sentimental" when she was twenty-six, but her life now was one of contentment, and she didn't want it interrupted by these hauntings.

The car swept up over a shallow hill, and the homestead came into view. The T-shaped farmhouse sat at the top of a sloping lawn whose summer grass was always faintly brown, except under the gnarled apple trees. The red roof was slightly swayback and the aluminum siding, she knew, covered solid logs. "Not a straight line in it," her father used to say, and she could never tell if he said it with irritation or with secret pride. From one corner of the house, an ancient fence made of uprooted stumps stacked with their roots interlacing wandered downhill toward the outbuildings. Among them, the dominant structure was the dairy barn, its wooden planks weathered to a pale bluish gray, its steeple roof towering above the hayloft where she and her brothers had walked across beams thirty feet over the threshing floor, pretending they were a high-wire act in the circus.

As the car turned into the graveled driveway, Fran felt her hand and arm go taut as she remembered what it felt like to touch those rough, splintered barn boards. Only yesterday she'd caressed the glassy surface of the newly refinished oak table which had been such a steal at an estate auction and which was just the right size for her telephone. "A very nice distressed antique," Julia had called it.

Her mother met her at the back door—within memory, no one had ever used the front door for comings and goings. Anna Himrich was a short, plump woman whose clothes were forever in eclipse behind the bibbed aprons she always wore, aprons made from a pattern handed down from her own mother. Her short, softly curling hair had begun to gray early, and now it was almost white. Her daughter's periodic insistence that coloring would make her look ten years younger was always answered with a smiling, "But I'm not ten years younger," and there the discussion would end.

"Frances," her mother smiled. "Come in." The sound of her full first name had an unfamiliar ring in Fran's ears. No one except her family ever called her that now, and she would tolerate it from no one else.

Anna's hands fluttered in front of her round body, telegraphing once again her uncertainty about whether she ought to embrace her daughter. Distressed and a little irritated as she always was by this uncertainty, Fran folded her mother in a hug that was warmly returned.

Fran couldn't pinpoint with any accuracy how and when it had begun, this distance. Certainly not when she'd gone away to college, an event without precedent in the family. Then, so homesick she couldn't eat, Fran had taken every opportunity to slip home on weekends where the circle closed comfortingly around her and the chatter went on into the winter nights long after the usual bedtime of the early-rising family. Back then, Anna had simply erased the absence which was to her so inexplicable, so unnecessary. Perhaps it had begun that Christmas vacation the second year of graduate school when Anna had found her packing on an icy December morning. From the doorway of the small room, her mother had said, "What are you doing? Vacation isn't over for another week," and Fran had answered, "I know, Mama, but I have two papers to do and the weather is clear, so I thought it would be a good time to start for home." At the last word, Anna had turned and walked quietly from the room. Yes, perhaps it had begun with something so small, but somewhere the circle was broken, and Fran had gradually come to see her life as a straight road leading away, always away.

Now, the embrace over, the two women walked without

touching each other into the large room which was both kitchen and dining room.

"Henry is here already," Anna said.

"I know. I saw the station wagon."

Fran frowned sideways at a littered desk table as she looked for a place to set down her bag; her eye caught a flash of silver.

"Isn't this the watch Paul gave Papa for Christmas?"

"Ya," Anna smiled apologetically, preparing an excuse for her husband.

"He broke it, didn't he?"

Anna nodded.

"That was an expensive watch, Mama. Why can't he keep a watch? He's broken dozens, lost scores."

"You shouldn't exaggerate, Frances."

"Well, I suppose it's symbolically appropriate," Fran said, tossing the watch back down again. "Papa never did have any sense of time."

Anna's face grew thoughtful. "I don't think that's quite true. He always came in when he got hungry, and we never had to wait meals for him. You remember that, don't you? He's just one of those people. He goes to bed when it's dark and he gets up when the sun comes up. And he doesn't need an alarm clock, either."

"Where's Paul, then? He certainly doesn't seem to have a built-in clock."

"Oh, I think it's the city traffic that holds him up."

Fran smiled inwardly. "The city" was Green Bay, not exactly a major metropolitan area.

Anna seemed to feel the need to change the subject.

"How was summer school?"

"Hot and tedious as usual. The regents still haven't released the money for our air-conditioning. And my students! I swear, only regular session failures ever go to summer school these days. It would be one thing if I could teach Goethe and Schiller all the time, but those beginning students—"

Fran broke off as she saw her mother's mild eyes drifting

toward the stove, and she realized that the question had only been Anna's way of asking, "How are you? Do things go well with you?"

"I'll go say hi to Papa and Henry. Where are they?"

"In the front room. Henry is being 'mysterious' again, but Papa knows, of course."

As the two women walked together to the other room, Fran glanced quickly at her mother's face; it was unchanged, as open and gentle as ever. Where did it come from, this calm knowing that asked few questions and never seemed to listen to the answers? Jacob Himrich came to meet them; he was a stocky, barrel-chested man whose graying hair framed a long, deeply lined face. His eyes, Fran suddenly thought, were the same bluish gray color as the barn doors.

"Frances," he said quietly, putting both hands on her shoulders. She leaned forward to kiss the crease between her father's eyes and turned to greet her older brother. Henry stood with his feet planted wide apart to balance the weight of his spreading torso. Six years as foreman at a local lumberyard had imparted an authoritarian air to his premature middle age, yet he always faltered slightly in his sister's presence.

"Well, Fran. We haven't seen you since Christmas."

"Easter, Henry. Easter."

"Oh, yeah. You brought chocolate bunnies for the boys." He smiled uncertainly. "Louise and the kids stayed in town."

Fran pictured the small frame house of which he was so defensively proud. Over Henry's shoulder, the massively framed portraits of their great-grandparents dominated one long wall: the man's unsmiling face; the woman's downturned face, aged before it was old. Between the portraits hung the gilt crucifix that had rested on the cover of Jimmy's casket. Jimmy, the brother who had died when Fran was eight, was never discussed; the Himrichs refused to dwell on their dead. Fran turned sharply to her mother.

"Mama, I thought you told me at Easter you were going to put those pictures in the attic." She could not include the crucifix.

"I will, I will," Anna laughed. "I know they're not very modern."

Fran sighed. "Come outside all of you and admire my new car."

They all trooped out into the yard, and Anna uttered exclamations over the now-soiled brilliance of the little car, speaking as always in these matters for herself and for Jacob. Henry leaned against his own station wagon, brooding downward over folded arms.

Fran looked past her brother at the small tractor parked near the east door of the barn. Without warning, the image sprang up before her eyes: the other tractor, her father's first. On that tractor, thirty-six years ago, her father had built an extra child-sized seat. Each of the boys in his turn had surveyed the farm from that perch before graduating to the driver's seat itself. This graduation was made into a real ceremony, with the family gathered and Jacob masking his pride by shouting counsel to the uncertain child maneuvering the jerking tractor around the yard, the huge, steel-lugged wheels digging down into the newly thawed earth.

The high-pitched, nasal chugging of a Volkswagen announced Paul's arrival. He stepped from the car, stretched up to his six feet, two inches, and smiled toward them. With his long body and stylish clothes, his thick chestnut hair and modish mustache, he looked a stranger among his short, thick family.

"Snappy car, Fran," he said. "I'm putt-putting around in Cindy's little buggy because my new one has been recalled. Something in the steering is haywire, they say." Then, before anyone else could speak, "Well, here we all are. What's for dinner, Mom?"

"Spareribs, sauerkraut, and dumplings."

"Oh, God! This ethnic cooking. Cindy says she'll have to let out all my suits if I eat here more than once a month."

"How is Cindy?" Fran remembered to ask.

"Oh, just fine. Getting more uncomfortable these last couple of months, that's all. She's home practicing her breathing exercises right now. The doctor says it's a textbook pregnancy. Everything is 'go' for the natural childbirth."

Fran saw Henry turn away with a look of faint distaste.

"Supper's almost ready to go on the table," Anna said, covering the silence.

Fran and her brothers sat at their old childhood places at the table. Combined with the absence of the wives and children, it made them all aware of something impending—some ritual that all expected and all were anxious to postpone. There was a great deal of chatter during the meal about the weather and teething children. In the silence which fell over coffee, Fran glanced at the bright yellow wall tile where four tiny holes remained as mute testimony to the childish rage which had made her fling a fork at Henry's smirking, superior face. No one ever alluded to it, but Jacob had never replaced the tile.

"How was the harvesting, Dad?" Paul said at last.

"Hard," Jacob said simply. "Peter couldn't help me as much as he thought he would be able to. And I don't have the machinery."

Henry saw his chance. "Of course it was hard, Papa," he said, "and it won't get any easier. You're sixty-six, after all."

Jacob turned his slow gray eyes and held his eldest son in a long glance.

"I know my age, Henry."

His son flushed hot. "Well, I couldn't get away from the mill to help you, Papa. I asked, but I just couldn't get away."

Fran and Paul exchanged glances in the embarrassed silence. Henry drew a ragged breath and reached for a cigarette. After a long drag, he began again more quietly.

"That's just what I've been trying to tell you all along. I can't help, and the college boy there—" He jerked his head at Paul and left the sentence unfinished. "Well, we aren't either of us farmers, Papa. I'm only thinking of you. It's time you sold."

The final syllable fell like a stone onto the table.

"Didn't take you very long to get to it, did it, Henry?" Fran said, an edge of bitterness coming into her voice.

"Now, Fran," he said, the cigarette smoke haloing his head. "You know I'm right, and you gotta help me talk to him. He can't keep on every year, planting and hauling and chopping, and this is a chance, such a chance."

"Talk to me, Henry, not to your sister." Jacob's voice was flat. "What exactly do you mean by 'such a chance'?"

"You know what I mean, Papa, so don't play it this way. Bill Connors told me about the new offer last week; it's better than last year's by twelve thousand. He wants all of it now because he knows that a housing development is a natural along the timber stand if there's going to be a golf course here."

"Golf." Jacob pronounced the word out of the corner of his mouth as he turned his head away. Into the single syllable, he packed all the disdain of countless generations for such foolishness.

"Papa, you gotta face it." Henry leaned forward. "The town is coming out to get you. Now sixty acres isn't much of a farm these days, but it's more farm than you can handle. And it's just right for this development. The county is going to blacktop the road next year."

"I suppose that has nothing to do with Connors's brother-in-law being on the county board, either," Jacob said drily.

"Well, Papa, one hand washes the other."

"*Must* you talk in clichés, Henry?" Fran sighed wearily. Henry shot her an angry glance before turning back to his father.

"This farm, Papa, with the woods and the pond, why it's just a natural for a golf course, and I know how you feel about golf so don't look that way. You gotta be realistic. Connors is willing to pay you *very impressive money*." Henry's right forefinger punched against the table to emphasize each of the last three words; a shower of cigarette ashes settled on the highly polished wood.

"I'm not impressed by Bill Connors's money," Jacob said, in the measured tones Fran remembered from all her days at home. He never spoke loudly, never quickly; even now, as he answered, he reached calmly to brush together the ashes that he knew were irritating his wife, just as he used to gather up the bread crumbs Henry would scatter around his plate to convince his mother he had eaten the crusts instead of shredding them.

"Well, you gotta be impressed by that much money." Henry was warming up now, and he stubbed out his cigarette in a saucer, reaching for another one at once.

"Not on the dishes, Henry!" Anna was indignant over the sacrilege committed on her mother's china. "I'll get you an ashtray."

"I'm sorry, Mama, but he makes me nervous talking about money that way. A farmer doesn't get a retirement pension, so what are you gonna live on with harvests getting harder and harder for him?"

"Talk to me, Henry." Jacob's voice was even quieter.

"All right, Papa, I am talking to you. I've been talking to you for three years, but let's face it, you never have been a practical man."

"Ah, the best and soundest of his time hath been but rash," Fran pronounced sarcastically, feeling at once the familiar sting of annoyance as they all turned blank, uncomprehending faces at her. "An allusion," she sighed. "Never mind." And they all turned away again.

"Paul, you talk to him." Henry spread his hands appealingly toward his younger brother.

Paul glanced at his father and faltered. Poor Paul, Fran thought. Of all of them, he was the most uncomfortable in this house. Handsome, amiable, and successful, at ease in his office where she'd once seen him with his long body flung back casually in the leather chair, he was nervous here, his face thrust forward in an earnest desire to please, but always thwarted, almost as if he and his parents spoke different, mutually unintelligible languages. His defense in any serious conversation was to agree with whoever had spoken last. He also had a wonderful trick of changing the subject with a shake of his thick hair and a flash of his perfect teeth. Football, the price of car repairs, the kids: these were his favorite topics during Sunday dinners at home. But this time, Henry was not about to be put off, or charmed, or distracted.

"Well, Paul," he insisted.

"Henry, I just don't know. If Dad doesn't want to sell, maybe we shouldn't try to push him. And he's doing all right so far, aren't you, Dad?"

"How the hell would you know how he's doing?" Henry snapped. "You don't even remember what the harvest is like. Don't you try to make me into the bad guy in this, just because I'm the only one who's ready to say what has to be said."

Watching Henry's angry face, Fran felt herself accused along with Paul, and she dodged the lash with her habitual retreat into irony.

"Dear Henry," she purred, "always the dutiful son." She took a grim satisfaction in seeing his face redden into deeper rage. But, as usual, helpless against her tongue, he turned back to his brother.

"Come on now, Pauly. You're the insurance actuary, so you know all about money and risks. You should tell him straight out what it means if he lets this chance go."

Paul shifted on the hard wooden chair and recrossed his long legs, sliding one hand along his expensive trousers.

"Well, Dad," he said without looking up. "Henry may be right. These are different times. It's not like the days when you could make a living with a Ten-twenty tractor and a team of horses. You and Mom need the security now, and Connors isn't going to wait forever."

Horses. As Paul talked on, Fran saw with startling clarity a long-buried image. She and her brothers, swathed to the eyes in coats and scarves, lay on their stomachs on a large, flat-bottomed sled, clutching the taut tie-ropes normally used to secure a load of hay. Her father towered above them with his feet braced against a board, leaning back into the reins, controlling with arms and shoulders the lumbering canter of the team. The brittle winter air echoed with delighted squeals as powdered snow and Jacob's laughter were whipped backward into the childrens' upturned faces.

The mare had been sold when Fran was seven and the placid, dun-colored gelding put out to pasture at last. When the gelding died two years later, Jacob had refused to sell his body for mink food but had buried the horse instead. It had taken him six hours on a muggy July evening to finish the job, and then he had never spoken of it again.

"Fran," Jacob interrupted Paul in mid-sentence. Startled from reverie, she looked up. There was a direct appeal in her father's eyes. "You haven't said anything."

And she knew she would have to say it at last, say what she thought she'd never have to say because the inevitable decision could be made without her, while she was away and wouldn't have to see it. She stalled for time, saying flippantly, "Well, I don't know, Papa. How many acres do you think I could do strapped to a plow?"

Jacob's face remained unchanged.

"This is not a game, Frances."

"Of course not," she sighed. "Nothing is ever a game to you, is it, Papa? Everything is always so serious."

She saw the wound strike home by the lowering of his eyes and the careful way he moved his fork to line up with the knife on his plate.

"I'm sorry, Papa," she said feebly. "I'm sorry. That wasn't fair."

And then Paul began talking again, smoothing things over, his horror of "scenes" moving him, almost, to eloquence.

Not fair, not fair. Of course not. There were the sleigh rides and the hayloft searches for newborn kittens when Jacob had held Henry's feet to prevent his getting stuck in the narrow passage from which the faint mewings came. And that bright Saturday summer morning when Jimmy had committed the unforgivable sin of tracking mud onto Anna's newly scrubbed kitchen floor: Anna standing on the back porch calling, "Jake! Jacob! You've got to do something about that boy," and her father, trotting in that odd way of his with his elbows held high and against his body, chasing Jimmy around the garage while she and Henry, dancing with excitement, cried from the hill, "He's coming the other way, Jimmy, he's coming the other way." Then the silence from behind the garage where father and son had met, broken at last by Jacob's roar of laughter and punctuated at intervals by Jimmy's breathless giggling, until at last, Anna too found her face crumbling into unwilling mirth before she turned back into her desecrated kitchen.

When had her father stopped laughing like that, Fran wondered; what had carved those lines into his face so that now he always looked serious? And what was at work on her own face — that line becoming steadily more visible between her brows? Vexation, disappointment, "nerves"?

Paul's chatter had ceased, and Jacob, immovable, said again, "Well, Fran?"

"I can't help you, Papa," she cried. "I can't farm the land. What do you want from me?"

"I want you to tell me what you feel about all of this," he said. "That's all I want."

Cornered, she felt cold anger. "I think you must sell, Papa, and I've thought so for a long time. The farm is too much for you and mother alone."

Jacob winced at the word "alone," and Anna made a quick gesture toward him, not touching him but putting her hand next to his saucer.

Ashamed, Fran softened her tone. "And this old house is so big. Mama should have things easier now, too. You could have a lovely apartment in town. Much more convenient, and think of how much fun you could have decorating and furnishing. Wouldn't that be nice? And making new friends? It must get lonely here for you now with everyone—"

She trailed off because Jacob was slowly turning his face away from her. The sight of the skin along his collar bone, as smooth and white as a baby's, filled Fran with an agonized tenderness.

"Papa, Papa. Forget the golf course. Why don't you sell the land to Uncle Peter so you and Mama can keep the house? Nothing much would be changed, but you wouldn't have to work so hard."

Jacob spoke from his averted face. "My brother, the gentleman farmer. I talked to him about that, but he tells me he's 'overextended.' "

"Uncle Peter said that?"

A sardonic smile twitched at the corner of Jacob's mouth. "I think it's his lawyer's word. Anyway, he's got so much money tied up in big machinery and new acreage, he can't see his way clear to invest more."

"Then sell the land to the development and keep the house and enough for your garden," she said.

"That's a good idea, Papa," Henry said, shooting a conspiratorial glance at Fran. She turned away in distaste.

"I won't stay here to look at strangers tramping around on my land," Jacob said, and though he didn't raise his voice, Fran recognized the finality of his tone.

"What's the difference, Papa, if the land has to go anyway?" Henry's anxiety was shrouding the table in cigarette smoke. "You're not making sense."

"Not to you, Henry," Anna said quietly. Forty years with Jacob had made a Himrich of her despite her soft mildness.

"You're right about one thing, Henry," Jacob said at last. "I'm tired, and there doesn't seem to be any other way."

After another pause, Jacob turned back to his children and said softly, "You make a very good living, Paul."

Paul jerked nervously to attention and looked around the table. "What do you mean, Dad?"

"You could afford a country house. It would be nice for you and Cindy and the kids in the summer, right next to the golf course."

Winter Roads, Summer Fields

All three children, puzzled at this latest turn, looked at their mother; it was a habit from their childhood. Often Anna had acted as translator when Jacob could not, or would not, say what he meant.

"It wouldn't be so hard for us to move," she said, "if the house stayed in the family."

Paul was stunned, out of his depth. "Gosh, it would be nice but this house—" He faltered. "Well, Cindy is used to more convenience. You know, a modern house and—and things. You know how women are, Dad." He grinned crookedly and fell silent.

"If I sell the land to the development, they will tear down this house."

There was an awful silence after Jacob's words. Anna spoke at last.

"His grandparents built this house."

"I know that, Mom. And I know you're fond of it," Paul said. "But it's not as if it were St. Peter's or something. It's an old house. It doesn't have that much property value."

"Yes, Mama, it's an old house," Henry said viciously, for he was angered by an old grievance. "But even if the property value is low, Papa would never think of asking me to buy it. I don't make a very good living like the college boy, do I? No, I went to work after high school so he could have his free ride to that good living."

"That's a typical *non sequitur*, Henry," Fran said drily.

"And that's another thing. The two of you. The educated ones. Always talking down to me. You, Fran, with your classy Ph.D., always sneering at Louise and me. You never ask me how *my* wife is. You two always had what you wanted, but I never got to go to college."

Fran's nerves finally gave way. "The truth is that you didn't go to college because you chose not to. You wanted to go right out and start cashing in on a big salary, and it *was* big in those days so don't snort. We never saw a dime of your money, Paul and I. And not Papa either. College! I'll tell you how Paul and I made it—on scholarships and grubbing at dirty summer jobs." She looked him in the eye. "And if you would speak truth in this house tonight, you would admit straight out that your real interest in this land sale is a tidy little estate for you to inherit."

"That is a dirty lie!"

Fran was moved to a little burst of hysterical laughter at the boyish phrase and the round-faced outrage she remembered so well from her childhood.

"It *is* a lie!" Henry raged. "I'm only thinking of them. But you! What have you ever done for this family? With your cushy job two hundred miles away. No responsibility for anybody except yourself. You're too high-class for the likes of us now, aren't you? Just who do you think you're kidding anyway, calling yourself Frankie and driving around in a foreign sports car? You should be embarrassed to go out on the street in it at your age."

Stung to tears, Fran said through her teeth, "Damn you, Henry."

"Enough." Jacob did not say it loudly, but his children recognized the tone. "This conversation is at an end. I'll call Connors tomorrow and say I'll sell it all. It has to be done."

He stood up heavily, pushing himself up with his hands against the old tabletop, and walked straight out the open back door.

Into the long silence that followed, Anna said musingly, "Jimmy would have been a farmer, I think."

Shocked at this unusual mention of their long-dead brother, the three children stared at their mother, who didn't look up.

"We have no way of knowing that, Mama," Fran said softly. "He was so young."

Anna sighed and stood up. "Now I should get at these supper dishes. It's getting dark already. The days are so much shorter again. Hard to believe that summer's almost over." And she began to collect the rose-covered dishes she used only for special occasions.

Ashamed, Fran began to help clear the table while Paul moved to the window and Henry reached for another cigarette.

"Henry, Henry," Fran said in a familiar, scolding tone. "You smoke too much. It's bad for you."

"I know, I know," he said. "I'm gonna quit one of these days."

Fran gathered knives and forks, thinking with guilty relief of returning the next day to her apartment to take delivery of the brown-and-gold striped love seat. Suddenly Paul turned from the window and said under his breath so that Anna, running hot water over the precious roses, would not hear, "Jesus, I can't stand it! He's just standing out there, leaning on the stump fence and looking out over the farm."

The brothers exchanged glances.

"Fran," Henry said softly. "Go out and talk to him. I was mad before, but you know you were always his pet. Come on, now, it's true."

Reluctantly, Fran handed the silverware to her brother and walked out into the gathering darkness. With the dew had come the fragrance of the earth, the dying heat of the brief northern summer clinging tenuously to the stubbled fields and the tangled tomato vines along the fence. When Fran came up to her father, he was resting both elbows in the smooth, upturned roots of one of the stumps, but he wasn't looking out over the farm. He was staring at the base of a sturdy old elm tree at the northeast corner of the house. Without looking at his daughter, he lifted one knotted hand and pointed at the tree.

"My grandfather died there," he said.

"What?" Fran started, feeling suddenly chilled in her thin summer blouse.

"On a Monday morning. He came home from the churchyard where he'd just buried Grandma. Asiatic cholera. He had it too, but he never let on. Didn't want to worry Grandma in her last hours. He made it that far and he died. When my pa found him, it looked like he'd just sat down against the tree to take a nap."

"I never heard that story before, Papa," Fran said. "I wonder why you never told us." She gazed past Jacob at the thickening darkness under the tree, feeling suddenly frightened and young, unaccountably young and childlike. "Imagine. Right there. My great-grandfather."

Jacob looked at her now, and she fell back before the concentrated bitterness in his face.

"My grandfather," he said and moved slowly back toward the house, his bull-like shoulders sagging forward as he walked.

Pulling Contest

(1987)

Luke Sensbauer was diffusing some of his anger by pounding as hard as he could on the metal feeder bin. The pounding was a signal for the calves all over the twenty-acre pasture to come to this shady corner for their food supplement ration. Luke was an old man, over seventy, but he still stood straight, his shoulders squared as if he were daring something to take him on, and the arm that swung the stick against the feeder did not tire easily. Only his clothes showed that he couldn't be a young farmer, for no one else would wear the baggy overalls and the wide-brimmed straw hat, though it was still possible to buy these things at the Farmers' Trading Company in the village. Luke Sensbauer seldom wore anything else and considered the modern caps very close to useless as protection against the summer sun. As for the tight-fitting jeans that his grandsons wore, and even his son, Tom, who was almost fifty and ought to know better, well, Luke was sure they were positively dangerous for farm work where it was important to be able to move your legs freely.

He liked calves, liked just to look at them, especially when they were a few months old and frisked around the pasture. His favorites were the Holstein-Hereford mix, with their smaller, blunter bodies and their nicely shaped heads. Nowadays, Holstein heifers were bred to a Hereford bull for their first calves because the lower birth weight made for easier labor. Later, the same cows would have Holstein calves to grow up into dairy cattle. Well, Luke thought, the Ag schools must be good for something, after all, because in his own days he'd often seen both heifer and calf die because of a difficult birth, especially if the labor started at night when there was no one around to help. And these little guys were really cute too, with Holstein markings and, usually, the reddish color of their papa. Watching them running toward him, Luke forgot for a moment and felt a little more cheerful.

He was angry partly with his grandson, Dennis, for what the boy had said to Tom, and partly with himself for standing there listening in when he should just have walked back out of the barn and gone about his business; he hated sneakiness of any kind and he felt as if he'd been sneaky, eavesdropping like that. He also felt betrayed. He actually turned the word over in his mind a couple of times, "betrayed." Because he'd always liked Denny best of all his grandsons, had the highest hopes for him. And he'd thought that the boy liked him too, appreciated the help he tried to give him in learning his way around farming. But there Denny was, standing in the silo shed doorway, saying those awful things to his father, when Luke had come into the barn from the east-side doors and had stopped short, unnoticed, to listen.

"I know all that, Dad, but I just wish you could get him off my back. He rides me all the time, like I was some kind of lazy hired hand or something."

"Come on, it's not that bad," Tom had answered from inside the silo shed where Luke couldn't even see him.

"It sure as hell is," Denny said, raising his voice even louder. "He bosses me all the time, and he acts like I don't know diddly about farming when he doesn't even know how to drive half the machinery we got."

"Well, he does know a lot about farming, young fella, and don't you forget it. I won't have you sassing your grandpa."

"I don't sass him. I never get to say anything at all to him because he just keeps on and on about how he used to do this and he used to do that."

"Well, he can't help it that times have changed. He likes to talk about the times when his ways were everybody's ways. You're family, so it doesn't hurt you to listen."

"But he's like that to all the hands, Dad. You wonder why we can't keep a herdsman for more than six months? It's because Grandpa is always after them too. You know what he said to Dan last year? He said, 'I guess you smart Ag school boys don't know everything, do you?'"

Inside the silo shed, Tom had chuckled softly.

"Listen, Denny. Dan left us because he finally got enough money together for a farm of his own, not because Pa ran him off."

"Well, you gotta talk to him anyway, Dad, because he's making me crazy."

Making him crazy. Hadn't he, Luke, taught that kid to ride a bicycle when his older brothers ignored him and Tom didn't have time for him? Hadn't he taken that kid to his silly high school football games and even stayed to cheer for him? And now he was making him crazy. Betrayed.

At the midday meal, Luke spoke to no one except to mutter "thanks" when Betsy, his daughter-in-law, passed him some food. He finished before the others and stalked back outside. Tom found him in the shade under the maple tree.

"So, how does the corn look to you, Pa?"

Luke gave him a sideways glance. So they were going to sneak up on it, were they?

"It looks great. Those hybrids are wonderful things, but we could use another good rain."

"Yeah, it's been a little dry lately."

There was a little pause, so Luke decided to take the offensive.

"You should quit that barn cleaner business and tend just to this farm, Tom."

"What makes you say that?" He looked really stunned.

"I don't know," Luke shrugged. "I'm getting too old to make it all run while you're gone most of the time."

"Has Denny been saying anything to you?"

"No, Denny doesn't say much to me." He couldn't keep the aggrieved note out of his voice.

"Listen, Pa. You know I got to keep turning a profit on the barn cleaner thing just to make the interest payments on all this." He made a sweeping gesture that took in barn, fields, cattle, and machinery. "And we got to have something to fall back on when the farm has a bad year."

Luke just grunted.

"And what's all this about you being too old, anyway? What brought this on? You're as hale as a hickory tree."

"Maybe it's just my ways is too old. All these big modern toys are beyond me."

"You been fighting with Denny, Pa?"

"No!" He said it a little too loud. "But that kid is getting to be a smart aleck."

"He's not a kid, Pa. He's twenty years old and he pulls his weight."

"You mean riding around the fields in that oversized buggy you call a combine, with its air-conditioning and that damned rock music so loud the Tomcheks can hear it clear the other side of the back forty? He could wreck the underside of that eighty-thousand-dollar rig and never know it, while he's deafening himself in comfort."

"If he hit something serious, the hydraulic system would lift the blades out of the way, and the warning light on the panel would come on."

Luke, who'd never ridden inside the combine, was stunned into silence for a moment by this piece of information. But it only seemed to make him more angry when he spoke again.

"I don't think it's natural, Tom. He can be in the field all day and he don't even get dirty. If he's fixing to be a real farmer, he should get some of his land on himself while he's working it."

"Whose rule is that, Pa? Where is that written down? You know that Denny really cares about the place, is interested in taking it over someday. We couldn't make farmers out of the other two, you remember. We lost them to the city and the paper mills, so we got to be glad that Denny takes an interest. Well, don't we?"

Luke turned his face away and gave no answer.

"Look here, Pa," Tom said, more gently. "I guess you and Denny are going through some rocky times right now, but what's most important here is that we keep this place moving along, and we got to work together for that. This is a family business, after all. It belongs to all of us."

"It ain't mine anymore," Luke said. "I'm just somebody who lives here."

"Now cut that crap, Pa," Tom said sharply. "This is Sensbauer land and it has been for more than a hundred years. You are the oldest Sensbauer around, so of course it's your farm."

"You got the deed."

"Yeah, and Denny will have it after me, if he wants it, but it'll still be my farm too."

Luke had developed a habit of deferring to Tom's opinions, and he couldn't help but see the reason in what he said now. When Luke spoke again, it was in a softened tone.

"It's just that everything is so changed. Farming used to be fun, and now it's just big business."

Tom laughed, a short, snorting laugh.

"Jesus, your memory is beginning to go, isn't it?" he said. "Cast your mind back, Pa. Farming was never fun. It was always damned hard work, even if you could love it like we did. And it was always a business, a family business, like I said before. What else is it when you make your living out of what you own?"

"Of course, that's true," Luke said. He was trying to be fair. "But you know what I mean. Some of these guys go only for the profit and loss. They don't really care about the land or about the life."

"Sure, there's guys like that. But they ain't us."

"But so much of it is slipping away. Jake Himrich had to sell his place for a golf course. And now you tell me them foreign investors want to buy Bill Seidl's farm for a tax write-off and then just let it lay there, going to weeds."

"Florida investors, Pa, not foreign investors."

Luke blinked twice, his face impassive.

"Same difference," he said at last.

Tom smiled broadly and touched his father's shoulder.

"Well, they ain't got us yet, Pa, and if we stick together, they won't get us ever."

Luke smiled back and then they both watched the fields for a while.

"I gotta go to Marshfield tomorrow to look at the new line of cleaner equipment," Tom said. "Denny is entering his mini-tractor in his first pulling contest over at Davister's. I'd like to see him drive, and I think he feels kinda bad that I won't be there. Maybe you could go along to see how he does."

"Uh," Luke grunted. It could have meant either "yes" or "no."

In the late afternoon sunshine, Luke stood outside the machine shed, having an argument with himself, readjusting the straw hat each time he changed sides. On the one hand, Tom was right about Denny's interest in the place, and probably he, Luke, was sometimes too hard on the boy, who, to give him his just due, was really a good kid. And it would be a shame if the boy had to go to Davister's track without his family backing him. On the other hand, this mini-tractor business was downright silly, and the boy had said some disrespectful things, even some untrue things, that very morning. Luke would never have dared to say such things about his own grandfather, because nobody would have allowed them to be said.

But as soon as he thought about his grandfather, Luke had to suppress the smile that began to turn up the corners of his mouth. The old man had lived to be ninety-four and was considered a genuine "character" for three counties around. And so he had been. He'd come from Germany as a boy not much older than Denny and had taken on the enormous task of clearing the eighty-acre farm that still formed the center of the present Sensbauer land. Having coped with that one high-risk change, he firmly resisted all other change for the rest of his life. He stubbornly refused to learn English, considered the earliest cars a passing fancy, and regarded air travel as a tool of the devil. When his son, Luke's father, had installed a telephone in the farmhouse, he had grumbled bitterly that it was *"ein verdammtes Ding,"* a damned thing. Only a few months later did the family learn from puzzled neighbors and relatives that the old man had learned one English sentence that he could use when the rest of the family was out of the house and the ringing of the phone was finally too much for him to stand. He would snatch down the receiver and bellow into the speaker, "Dis is Heinrich Sensbauer; you vant to talk to me, you come to mein house." Then he would hang up.

Well, Luke thought to himself, maybe his grandfather wasn't the only one who had trouble with change. He settled his hat more firmly onto his head and walked into the machine shed. He wanted to be fair, after all.

Denny was painting black stripes onto the white fenders of his mini-tractor, the finishing touches before tomorrow's contest. With his cousin, Bob Heim, Denny had built the engine and put together the frame of the machine he'd named "the Gambler," and he was very proud of it. To Luke, the tractor looked like some oversized toy, its large rear wheels coming only just above Denny's waist, the front wheels looking like they'd come off a baby buggy. All of the exposed engine was painted silver, and the chrome exhaust pipes, which pointed straight up on either side of the manifold, were not much taller than Luke.

Denny was concentrating on keeping the flow of paint even between the two strips of masking tape, but he'd seen his grandfather come into the shed. He was a nice-looking boy, Luke thought, well built and clean-shaven, but his blond hair was too long, almost in his eyes, and those jeans—any tighter and he wouldn't be able to bend over. Luke walked all around the little tractor before speaking.

"Where's the radiator?" he asked.

"Doesn't have a radiator," Denny said without looking up.

"What cools the engine, then?"

"Nothing cools the engine. It only runs for two or three minutes, so it just gets hot. It can cool down later. A radiator would add too much weight."

Luke snorted.

"It can only run for two minutes and it's the size of a calf. What a waste of money and gas."

"It doesn't use gas," Denny said, cool as well water. "It runs on alcohol."

"Sounds dangerous."

"It is. That's why I got this fire extinguisher built in here." He leaned over to pat the bright red cylinder.

Luke frowned, his already-creased brow folding over itself as a knot of fear twisted in his stomach. His own brother had died in a fire.

"What the hell is this thing good for, anyway?" he growled. "Now, mind you, I think a pulling contest is a good thing. We always had 'em, first with horses and later with tractors. But we used to have some purpose for 'em, to test our animals or our machines, the same ones we used every day on the farm. There was some practical purpose to the whole thing."

Denny looked up for a second, the brush hanging from his hand, and his face was half-amused, half-scornful.

"Come on, Grandpa. A contest is a contest. It ain't about 'practical.' It's about seeing who can win."

"But we didn't waste time and money building toys like this."

"I got the time and the money is mine," Denny said coldly and went back to painting.

"Just so you don't kill yourself over the fool thing."

After a long pause, Luke made another circuit around the Gambler and reached out to trace his finger over some of the wiring.

"You better not touch anything, Grandpa," Denny said without looking up. "Bob had to drive all the way to Kenosha for some of those parts."

"Really? How far is that?"

"Almost three hours."

"I mean, how many miles is it?" Luke said, irritation coming back into his voice.

Denny looked up with the kind of blank expression he sometimes had when his grandfather said something he couldn't see the sense of.

"I don't know. You could look at a map or something, I guess." His voice was calm as he bent to his painting once more.

Again, an uncomfortable pause followed, and Luke folded his arms inside his overall bib.

"Yes, sir," Luke said at last. "Pulling contests really used to be something. The horses were the best. We used to talk about the contest weeks ahead of time. Every Sunday after church, we'd cross the road to Smeester's tavern and try to find out about all the teams."

"Smeester's?" Denny looked up in surprise. "The same tavern that's there now?"

"Sure, the same building. Different owner now, of course, and it's all changed inside. Oh, you should have seen it in my day. It had a polished floor and a pressed tin ceiling. You don't see that—"

"I thought you were going to tell me about the horse pulling contests."

Luke had a stunned look on his face. Then he snapped, "You're the one who asked me about Smeester's, aren't you?"

"Sorry," Denny murmured, and Luke decided it was best to go on as if Smeester's hadn't been mentioned.

"We'd have 'em at the fairgrounds, make a real picnic out of it. George Saeker would bring his stone boat and we'd load on the stones, not too many at first, and then every team had a turn. Gradually, we'd pile on more and more stones and the teams would start to get eliminated. That was the real test of strength, not like them computerized sleds you got nowadays."

"They're not computerized, for God's sake. It's just simple hydraulics. The more the weight moves forward, the harder it is to pull the sled. And the weight can be measured exactly."

"Well, next year, they'll be computerized for sure. Anyway, like I was saying, towards the end, when there were only about four teams left, the pile of stones was higher than the horses. You shoulda seen 'em, leaning into the harnesses, practically digging themselves down to China with them big hooves, muscles standing out in their necks."

"Sounds kinda hard on the horses."

"No, no. They was bred to pull, liked it. Peter Kollross had a pair of silver Belgians that was beautiful to look at. They won almost every year, till Pete sold 'em off to buy his first tractor."

"Did you ever win, Grandpa?"

"Nope. Came close a coupla times, but my team wasn't as big as them Belgians."

"Big isn't always best," Denny said, patting the wheel next to him and smiling slyly at his grandfather.

"Hmph," Luke snorted, but it was hard to tell what he meant because he smiled afterwards.

It was a hot day and the temporary bleachers were already full by the time Luke got to Davister's track. Denny had taken the pickup around behind a barrier where other drivers would help him unload his mini-tractor. Luke found himself a place to stand along a snow fence that had been set up to mark off the track from the field around it. Off to his left was a stand with a microphone and loudspeaker.

Ron Davister had sold off most of his land for a housing development, but he still had about fifteen acres where he raised saddle horses for sale. And he had set aside this place behind his barn for tractor pulling contests. The track was a quarter-mile path cut out of the sod. The dirt was raked smooth for the start of the truck pulling, which came first.

Luke thought the customized trucks looked ridiculous, the pickup bodies perched high above wheels so huge and so wide-set that the fenders couldn't possibly cover them. The trucks were painted in bright colors and covered with advertisements for local businesses and garages. When the first truck was hooked up to the weighted sled and set into roaring motion, it was clear what the day was going to be like. The truck's whirring tires bit into the dry ground, sending clouds of reddish brown dust twenty feet into the air. The wind was from the northeast, sending the clouds straight over the spectators.

Luke got a few muffled laughs out of the trucks. Twice, the flashy, bucking machines pranced up to the sled only to have their drive shafts ripped out several seconds later, before they'd pulled the sled fifteen feet.

"Damned idjits," Luke said to no one in particular, feeling very satisfied.

The full-size tractors came next and this was something Luke could enjoy despite the buildup of grit in his nose and mouth. Some of the tractors were vintage models, old John Deeres whose two huge cylinders gave them that familiar "putt-putt" sound, and even an old Oliver 88 just like the one Luke had once owned. Olivers were good tractors, Luke thought happily, and he was pleased when the 88 won second prize in its class.

The mini-tractors were last because this was the most popular event, and Denny would be the last contestant because he was a late entrant. By that time, the track would be as torn up as it could get. Luke began to feel depressed again. The sun was hot on his shoulders. Someone touched his arm, and when he turned, he saw Denny holding out a sweating bottle of beer.

"Thought you could use this," Denny said and was walking back through the crowd before Luke could think of what he wanted to say to the boy.

Luke drained the beer before the announcer had finished naming the first contestant in this last competition. The mini-tractor, painted bright red, was towed out onto the track by Lloyd Liebeck's pickup. Luke remembered what Denny had said about the engines running for only two or three minutes without radiators, so he guessed they couldn't be started at all until they were ready to begin pulling. The pickup bounced off to the side of the track and a towrope was stretched between the little tractor and the sled. The driver's head was hidden inside a motorcycle helmet with a dark windscreen across the face. Someone shouted, "Tear 'em up, Hank," and a pattering of applause spread through the bleachers just before the engine started with a sound like a small explosion. The big wheels began to spin instantly and the whole front part of the tractor bucked up into the air like a rearing horse. In a few seconds, the engine was making a high-pitched screaming sound and the tractor had disappeared in a cloud of brown dirt. The cloud moved forward, fast enough at first, and then slower and slower as the weight moved toward the front of the sled. Finally, the little front wheels dropped out of the cloud and the noise stopped as abruptly as it had begun.

Men rushed toward the machine, one to mark the place where the wheels had dropped, one to unhook the towline, and one to record the weight. The crowd was still applauding while the pickup truck towed the mini-tractor off the track. It had been a good first run, hard to beat, the announcer said, as a tractor dragged the sled back to its starting position.

One by one, the mini-tractors were announced, their names taken from country and western songs or just from local taverns which had sponsored them, their drivers representing both families Luke had known all his life and names he'd never heard before. Each time the expectant hush was broken by the screaming engine, and each time the dirt whirled upward as if a bomb had erupted from under the ground. Some of the tractors bucked to a stop almost as soon as they started, their customized engines hopelessly flooded. Others churned forward almost to the marks made by the first entry, excitement building in the crowd each time one came close.

Luke found himself caught up in the excitement, urging some of the tractors forward just because their drivers were named Kollross or Ashenbrenner. After the sixth entry, he took out his big, white pocket handkerchief and held it over his mouth and nose, for he was beginning to think he might choke to death before Denny's turn came around. The eighth tractor started out sluggishly, its wheels seeming to move in slow motion. Suddenly the driver threw his arms in front of his face as a liquid began spraying up from the engine; it was the alcohol fuel. The crowd gasped as little flashes of fire danced over the hot surface of the engine wherever drops of alcohol landed. Two men rushed forward with fire extinguishers already fogging the air in front of them, and the fires were instantly killed. The driver waved gamely, though a bit sheepishly, to cheering spectators as his tractor was towed away. Luke lifted his handkerchief back to his mouth, but his grime-encircled eyes had grown narrow and worried.

Finally, the announcer was saying, "And the last entry is newcomer Dennis Sensbauer on the Gambler, built by the driver and his cousin, Robert Heim." The tractor appeared, and Luke felt a flash of irritation when he saw that the white fenders had already been coated by the drifting dust, making the tractor look a little shabby. Denny sat rigidly upright, his bare hands clutching the steering wheel as if he was already urging the tractor forward. He had pushed his hair up inside a billed cap bearing the name of the garage where Bob worked. The sled rope was attached and the tow truck moved away. Luke pressed the edges of the handkerchief against the sides of his face until he could feel his teeth beginning to hurt.

Denny's right hand moved and the engine exploded into sound, the wheels churning, the front end bucking. Then Denny disappeared into the cloud of dirt as all the other drivers had done. The sled moved surprisingly quickly at first and the crowd, dazed into silence by three hours of heat and dirt and noise, began to stir a little. As the sled started to slow, the screaming of the engine became louder, and a sudden gust of wind let everyone have a brief glimpse of the back wheels, still churning madly, the rubber treads clawing down into the trenches made by the other tractors. The noise of the crowd began to build. Luke had neither moved nor made a sound.

Now the tone of the engine began to come down as the numbers of revolutions slowed toward the inevitable stall. But still the sled inched forward, and still the cloud of dust crept toward the announcer's stand. The sound of the motor had quieted enough so that the cheering from the bleachers rose above it. The tractor was moving so slowly now that the cloud of dust was shrinking around it. By the time the engine growled to a stop and the front wheels fell to the ground for the last time, the dust had cleared enough so everyone could see that Denny had passed the marks made by the first tractor.

The crowd noise was almost deafening and the announcer's voice over the loudspeaker had an hysterical ring to it. Luke let go of his own face for the first time since Denny's tractor had come out onto the track. His voice was just a hollow croak as he tried to shout with the crowd, so he snatched his big straw hat off his head and threw it to the ground. Then, because that somehow didn't seem enough, he danced up and down on the hat, smashing the crown level with the brim, trampling all of the pale straw into the swirling dust.

Denny had jumped down to see for himself where his wheels were being marked. Now he stood up straight, grabbed his cap in his right hand, and waved it at the bleachers. Then he lifted both of his arms above his head, dancing in a half circle until he could see Luke against the snow fence. The boy's hair was plastered against his head. Upward from the line of his cap, his pale forehead gleamed in the afternoon sun; below the line, his face was dark brown, completely covered in dirt. With his arms still aloft, he began to run toward his grandfather, whose own arms were now thrust out in front of him, the soiled handkerchief dangling unnoticed from his right hand.

Tree House

(1990)

The box elder tree stood in the corner of a small field on the
Mueller farm, just to the east of the house and about twenty feet
from the road. It was a "volunteer," a tree that had simply
sprouted there one summer and had been allowed to remain, a
harmless intruder in the pasture that was no longer used for
regular crops. In twenty years, the tree had grown to an impressive
size, its stout trunk supporting a wide canopy that rose up from
the two major branches—each as big around as the trunk of a
smaller tree—which forked away to north and south just four feet
above the ground. In the summer, the dark leaves were so dense
that it was impossible to see through the tree even when the wind
should have been opening occasional pathways for light.

On a cool early summer day, Jim Mueller stood beneath the
tree looking up into the branches, drawn there by an idea that had
been coming back into his head from time to time all winter. Each
time he'd glanced out his bedroom window to check the weather,
the naked winter branches had drawn the idea back into his
consciousness, and when spring brought the first leaves, he'd
almost formed the idea into a resolution. Now he circled the tree
twice, looking up. Finally, he stretched out on his back, the pale,
new grass feeling cool through his denim jacket. From this vantage
point, it was easier and more comfortable to study the tree's
possibilities.

It had been a hard winter for Jim Mueller and not just the
weather, though heaven knows, that had been bad enough—
twenty-three below zero on Christmas Day, cars choking to a stop
on the road because their gas lines had frozen while they were
moving. But the winter had also brought three changes into Jim's
life. He had turned fifty-four on March 27, remembering with a
shudder that he had once, and not too long ago, considered fifty

Winter Roads, Summer Fields

old. He and his wife had marked their thirtieth wedding anniversary in April by moving into a two-bedroom ranch house across the road from the house where he and his father before him had been born. The ranch house was so new that some of the electrical outlets still had no covers. And he had turned the management of the farm over to his son, Bill. At twenty-seven, Bill was ready to stop being a hired hand; he and his wife, Lee Ann, had three children now and needed the space of the big house.

"You and Mom deserve some time off," Bill had said cheerfully. "Fly to Vegas every now and then, visit Barbara in California. Except for spring planting and bringing in the harvest, I can handle things around here."

And Jim knew it was true. Even a big dairy operation like theirs had become so automated that manpower was no longer very important. But Jim didn't tell his son how he really felt about turning visits to his daughter and gambling junkets into a life's work. He didn't think he could make the boy understand that he didn't feel old at all, didn't feel like tapering off toward an early retirement. Even Jim's wife didn't seem to understand when he tried to tell her that he felt like starting all over again, maybe at some other job.

"Muellers have always been farmers," she said.

That was certainly true. Jim had taken over the homestead when he was much younger than Bill was now, because his father's health had failed early. Matthew Mueller's sturdy appearance hid the fact that he had severely damaged kidneys from being gored by a bull. He'd begun walking with two canes when he was younger than Jim was now, and he had died at fifty-nine. So Jim had never seriously considered what else he might have done with his life; the choice had been made for him by one of those realities of farm life—an otherwise docile animal gone suddenly crazy while Matt Mueller was crossing a field he had believed was safe. If Jim had thought that he might like to try his hand at building things, even at inventing things, there was no money in those days for the schooling and, besides, farming eventually made amateur builders, electricians, inventors, and engineers out of any men who stayed in it long enough—pure necessity became the teacher.

But Jim had always felt thwarted by the piecemeal nature of that work—it was always a response to some crisis, or else it was a partial remodeling of some existing system or building. He'd never designed or built anything "from scratch" as his wife did with her recipes, which were famous throughout the county. Now his restlessness, his growing feeling that he was expendable on the farm, made him think that other people must make choices about their lives, not just have things *happen* to them all the time. And he'd begun to think he wanted to build something, all by himself, with no help from anyone, something that was not for cows, or tractors, or extra feed space. The impulse had brought him here, lying flat on his back under the box elder tree.

"Are you drunk or sick or what?"

The voice was so near that Jim sat straight up in surprise. When he turned his head, he saw a tall, gaunt old woman standing about six feet behind him. She was wearing a bright yellow blouse and a plaid skirt; a purple scarf was wrapped around her thin neck and then draped down almost to her waist. Her sharp-featured face was shaded by an immense hat with bright silk flowers attached to the crown, sprays of leaves extending almost to the edge of the straw brim.

"Celie Lanzer," Jim blurted.

"That's who I am, all right," she said, "but it doesn't answer my question. What's wrong with you? I saw you from the road, laying there like you were dead or something. I had to walk around to your gate."

"I'm all right," he said, getting to his feet. "I was studying this tree, that's all. I'm thinking of building a tree house in it."

She lifted her face to look up into the branches, and the light was let in under the hat brim. Her face was drawn, deeply lined, but her eyes were clear and bright, like a young woman's eyes.

"Why do you want to do that?" she said, bringing the shadow back down over her face.

"For my grandchildren," he lied. "I got three grandchildren."

"I know," she said. "I see them in church. Your boy married the Krieger girl. I was in church for the wedding."

Celie Lanzer had gone to every church ceremony as long as Jim could remember; she always sat in the back, and everyone had grown so used to having her there that they hardly noticed her anymore.

"Aren't you cold, walking way out here without a coat?" Jim asked.

"No," she said, adjusting the purple scarf. "This is June, isn't it? Besides, walking fast is warm work." Her voice sounded husky, muffled, as if she were not used to speaking.

"Well, I'm all right, as you can see," Jim said, after a little pause, at a loss for anything else to say to her. In all his life, this was the first time he'd ever spoken to Celie Lanzer.

"A tree house," she said with a little shake of the silk flowers. Then she turned abruptly and walked off toward the gate in the familiar loping stride that everyone in the county recognized.

It wasn't odd that Jim had known who Celie Lanzer was all his life without ever talking to her. He suspected that was the case with most of the people in Hammern who would say they knew her. She was both a local institution and a local puzzle. Jim's father had pointed her out to him when he was just a child, but she was very different then—a thin, quiet young woman who appeared in church on Sundays with her mother. Her father had died when she was nineteen and her brother, Nick, had moved away to Michigan somewhere with his wife and children; people said that he later left his family, just disappeared one day, and even his mother didn't know where he was.

The Lanzer farm went into a slow decline, the two women doing their best with a series of hired men. Everyone said that Celie worked as hard as a man herself, but she and her mother just got poorer and poorer. One by one, the Lanzer fields were left to go fallow, and the cows were sold off, only a few kept for milk and meat. When her mother fell ill, Celie came to church alone, grown even more quiet, more plain and dowdy-looking.

It was inevitable that she should become an object of fun for the parish boys, who made faces behind her back, then aped courtly behavior by rushing ahead to hold doors for her and bowing from the waist when she passed them. If she heard the giggles behind her, she never let on. Everything about her then seemed drawn in, even the way she walked, her large feet seeming to make a minimum of movement when she set them one in front of the other.

One Sunday when Jim was fifteen, he'd witnessed Celie's one break in composure. His cousin, Philip Mueller, had sidled up behind her at the holy water fountain and whispered something in her ear. She had blushed, immediately and violently, and then whirled to look at him.

"You deceitful sinner!" she cried in a clear, ringing voice. "Hell is too good for you!"

It took a moment for the laughter to begin, but not long enough to allow Celie to get out of the church without hearing it. She returned to her quiet, mousy behavior but, of course, the speech had instantly passed into local folklore, producing a chuckle whenever it was repeated. Celie was already a "character," though she couldn't have been much older than thirty at the time.

Her mother lived a long time, lingering in her illness until everyone felt sorry for Celie who was "devoting her life to that sick old woman," while the Lanzer farm deteriorated into the worst eyesore in the county. The power company even shut off the electricity eventually, so Celie and her mother went back to living the way people had in the twenties. Celie passed almost imperceptibly into middle age and then late middle age, always looking the same, seen only in church and at the grocery store. But Mrs. Lanzer finally died, and the day after her funeral, Celie sold the farm. The boom of the sixties had inflated the price of farmland, so everybody knew what a good price she'd got for it, despite the condition of the place.

Winter Roads, Summer Fields

Celie moved into an apartment in the village, and the transformation in her was almost instantaneous. She began to appear in bright, almost outlandish clothes. Her hats, especially, became the subject of local gossip. In winter, she wore expensive felt hats with large brims; these hats were always trimmed in feathers: pheasant feathers, peacock feathers, even ostrich plumes. In the summer, she favored straw hats in every pastel color, trimmed with ribbons, flowers, and plastic fruit. Local women joked that Celie must have a special hat catalog because such hats were never shown in the local stores.

And Celie began her walks. She would head out of the village and walk for hours along country roads, her stride lengthening into one the local wags called "Celie's gallop." She'd been reported as far as five miles from town, loping along the shoulder of the road in her bizarre clothes, looking for all the world like some tall, exotic bird, a flightless bird always in a hurry. This had been going on for so long that a whole generation of local girls had grown up listening to their mothers say, "Must you walk like Celie Lanzer?" whenever their gait was something less than ladylike.

In recent years, Celie had developed a new habit, one that kept local drivers on the alert. She would glance over her shoulder at the sound of an approaching car and then, without breaking stride, dart across the road in front of it, almost as if she had devised some private game of "chicken," seeing how close she could come to being run down. Of course, most people said she had "gone simple," and the more cautious parents pulled their children out of the way when Celie swept past them in church, trailing bright scarves and a whiff of cheap perfume.

So Jim hadn't really been very surprised that Celie had appeared like this, two and a half miles from the village. He too had grown used to seeing her on country roads. But he was amazed that she'd spoken to him. He realized that he could add to local legend by reporting her question—"Are you drunk or sick or what?"—but he felt disposed to keep it to himself. Partly he didn't want to explain why he'd been lying under a tree, and partly he felt that Celie had meant him a kindness, which gossip would ill repay.

Jim began his project the next day, scrounging pieces of lumber out of the machine shed. His first step was to build a ladder that would be permanently attached to the tree. The trunk and one of the two main branches provided the perfect slant for such a ladder and Jim had it installed before the day was over. That evening, at supper, he told his wife what he was up to. She smiled and said, "Good. That should keep you out of mischief for a while."

For two more days, Jim spent time up in the tree, studying. He even sawed out some branches. Then he went into town to buy his supplies: lumber, clamps, and cable. Bill became curious and asked him about it.

"It's no big deal," Jim said. "I just want to give my grandchildren somewhere to play, and I want to do it by myself. I'd appreciate it if you didn't try to help."

"I wasn't volunteering, Pa," Bill chuckled. "I got plenty to keep me occupied right now."

On Saturday, Jim was cabling an eight-by-eight beam against the branches of the tree, working with his feet braced against neighboring branches, when Celie appeared on the road. She came to a stop and stood for a moment, watching. Jim pretended he hadn't seen her and went on working. But she crossed to the gate anyway and came to stand under the tree, in its shade, about six feet to the south of where Jim was working.

"Why do you need such a big beam?" she said in her muffled, unused voice.

"It's a base for the floor," he said grudgingly. "I don't want the house itself to be actually nailed to the tree anywhere."

"Why not?"

"It's always windy here, up on the ridge like we are," he grunted, leaning forward to wrap more cable. "Sometimes the wind just lashes this tree around. If the house is nailed to the tree, it'll splinter apart in the first good blow. All my work will be for nothing. So I'm gonna rest the floor on this eight-by-eight. That way, the house can slide back and forth on it when the wind shakes the tree. There'll be another one over there for the other side." And he lifted his hand to point, feeling a little surprised at himself for having said so much.

The gaunt figure below him moved around to the other side of the tree and then back again.

"The branches over there don't look very strong," she said. "Are they going to be able to support the weight?"

Jim paused and looked over at the branches.

"You could be right," he murmured.

"What?"

"You could be right, I said. Maybe I could suspend that beam by cables from above. I'd have to make the house about two feet narrower, but then it could sway on that side like a hammock. Yeah, that might be better." He scratched at his chin with the end of the cable, forgetting for a moment that Celie was there.

"I'll be getting along now," she said, and loped away before he could answer.

She came every third day after that, except for Sundays, almost as if she'd set up a schedule. While June turned into July and the hot weather came on, Jim saw a succession of hats appearing below him as he suspended a platform, cut a hole in it at the top of the ladder, and began to frame up the walls. Celie began to wear only white dresses, though they were still trimmed with bright scarves, belts, and flowers. Every time she came, she asked questions about the house, and Jim answered them as he went on working.

Other people came to watch him too—his wife, Bill and Lee Ann, their kids. One day, Lee Ann's father, Roy Krieger, stopped his pickup on the road and walked over with his youngest son to "see what's going on." Each time these people came to watch, Jim would stop working, climb down, and change the subject to the weather, the bank's baseball team, anything to keep from discussing what he was doing up a tree. Yet with Celie, he began not to mind answering her questions. It was almost like thinking out loud, and it helped him to make changes in his design, improvements, as he went along.

One day in late July, when Celie had stayed a little longer than usual, Jim did climb down for a little rest.

"Why do you walk so much, Celie?" he asked, half in exasperation, half in real curiosity.

She lifted her hat brim to look at him, her clear, direct gaze a little disconcerting.

"It's better exercise than going to funerals," she said shortly.

"I know what you mean," Jim chuckled ruefully. "Seems I'm spending more time than I used to going to funerals too. At my age, people you know are starting to die."

"I go to all the funerals," Celie said. "And the weddings. And I stay after church to watch the baptisms too."

After that, Jim began to bring two glasses out with his thermos of lemonade on the days he was expecting Celie. Most of the time, she would drink a glass by herself while he worked, shaping the roof and carrying up the leftover roll of garage roofing that he'd kept in the machine shed. Occasionally, though, he would climb down to have a drink with Celie, telling her all about what he was doing that day.

"How old are you?" she said abruptly on one such day, looking at him with one of her direct stares.

"Fifty-four," he said, feeling oddly embarrassed by the intrusion of a personal question.

She looked out across the field, her hawkish features profiled against the fading afternoon light.

"I was just a little younger than that when my mother died," she said. "After that, I didn't have anything to do."

After a long pause, Jim said, "It's a heck of a time to have to start over, isn't it?"

"Yes," she said, setting down her glass and preparing for one of her sudden flights, "a heck of a time."

When Jim had finished the roof, he installed two hinged windows on each long side wall, windows that hooked up to the ceiling to let breezes through, but closed down with bolt locks to snug in the interior. The house was six feet by eight feet and the roof was high enough for even a tall adult to stand upright in the middle of the floor. When he'd got this far, Jim was almost out of ideas. He'd lashed the major branches together with steel cable so that they couldn't spread outward and allow the house to fall off its one eight-by-eight runner. His suspension of the other long side had worked beautifully. He was confident of the stability of the house, and he'd treated all of the wood on the outside with wood preservative-stain that made it almost the same color as the tree trunk.

One hot day in early August, Jim walked all around the tree in increasingly widening circles. He was pleased to see that, despite its size, the house was not visible through the thick canopy unless he was standing almost directly beneath the tree. From the road, where he was now standing, even the ladder couldn't be detected. It gave him a great deal of satisfaction to know that his design had resulted in what he knew was one of the chief virtues of a tree house—secrecy.

Celie appeared almost at his elbow, having approached noiselessly in the soft grass along the ditch. Her dress was white with red polka dots, her shoes were red, and the white boater was trimmed in a wide red ribbon.

"Is it finished?" she asked. They had long ago dispensed with greetings, and Celie never waited for farewells when she bolted away.

"I'm not sure," Jim replied. "I guess it could use some finishing touches inside, painting maybe, but I think it's mostly done."

"May I see it?" she asked, very formal, like a schoolteacher. "Inside, I mean?"

Jim hesitated. He felt oddly possessive about the tree house and wasn't sure he wanted anyone to see it just yet. And, despite her almost daily exercise, Celie was surely over seventy years old. Could he be sure she wouldn't slip in those ridiculous shoes and break her hip?

"Unless you would rather I didn't see it," she said, already moving away.

"No, no," Jim protested, and he almost reached out to take her arm. "It's all right. It's just that I'm worried about you climbing in those shoes."

"I'm fine," she said, lifting her head to a lofty angle, her sharp eyes already on the ladder. "I'm not like those fragile women, you know."

"All right," Jim said, "but I'll go up behind you, just in case."

He didn't know if it was the light or some reflection from her red ribbons, but Jim thought for a moment that Celie might be blushing. She swept past him in that paratrooper stride of hers and was halfway up the ladder before he could get to the tree. When he hoisted himself into the tree house, Celie was already standing in the center of the floor with her hands on her hips.

"Not bad," she said when he looked at her. "But now you have to think like a child for the last touches."

"How?" he asked.

"There," she said, pointing at the opening in the floor. "You'll have to put a railing around that hole or some child is going to fall through it and get seriously hurt. Can't have that happening to your grandchildren."

"You're right," he said, remembering how careful Lee Ann always was about the kids. "That's a good suggestion."

"Over there," she said, pointing to the narrow south wall. "You need a table and some chairs so the kids can play games."

Jim looked back at the two-foot-square hole he had just climbed through.

"I could get chairs in, I suppose," he said, "but I can't get a table through that hole." He felt irritated at himself for not having thought of getting other things into the house once it was finished.

"You can build a table," she said. "If you design it right, you can make it so it folds up against the wall like these windows. Then the children could use the whole floor again if they wanted to, maybe with blankets for sleeping."

"Sure," he said. "I could attach one edge to the wall and have hinged legs on the other side. It would fold up nice and snug, wouldn't be in the way at all." Immediately he felt excited about the table. He walked past Celie to measure quickly with his hands.

"No, shorter than that," Celie said from behind him. "Those children are not as big as you are."

Jim went on with his measuring, but he moved his hands about six inches further down. When he looked up again, it was just in time to see Celie's boater disappearing below the opening in the floor.

The railing and the table took Jim the better part of two weeks because he had to take some time off to help Bill make second-crop hay. Celie didn't show up in all that time, and Jim began to worry about her. Could she be sick? He seriously considered calling someone in town to find out what had become of her, but he realized how silly that would sound. He wouldn't even be able to explain it to his wife.

At the end of the second week, Jim was painting the inside walls of the tree house when he heard a voice under the tree.

"James Mueller?"

It was the first time Celie had used any name for him at all. He wiped his hands on the legs of his trousers and hurried down the ladder.

She was dressed in a white blouse and a blue, floral-print skirt. Her hat looked like something out of *Gone with the Wind*— a wide-brimmed white straw with a royal blue scarf wrapping the crown and bending the edges of the brim almost to Celie's ears before tying in a floppy bow under her chin. She was holding a package wrapped in brown paper.

"I brought something," she said, looking down at her hands, "for the house."

Jim was at a loss for words but took the package when she thrust it at him.

"The small windows, the ones that don't open," Celie said. "They could use some curtains. And I think there's enough there to make a cloth for the table too. I heard you pounding inside the other day, so I guess you made a table. Your wife can sew, can't she?"

"Yes," Jim murmured. "She can sew."

His mind was racing. The tree house was his, and he'd never imagined it with curtains. Besides, he could only guess what outlandish fabric Celie Lanzer might think appropriate for curtains. The package felt heavy in his hands.

"Well," she said from beneath the shadow of the hat brim. "Open it."

Automatically, Jim wiped his hands against his trousers to make sure his fingers had no more wet paint on them. Then he tore the paper open across its long seam. The fabric inside burst from its packing into the hot afternoon air, bringing with it the strong smell of cedar. It was a heavy, stiff linen, cream-colored with a fine stripe of dark beige running through it at intervals of about three inches. Jim put his fingers down onto the rich cloth, hardly daring to believe it was real.

"I've had it since I was a girl," Celie said. "My father gave it to me when I was eighteen. It was the middle of the Depression and he couldn't afford it, but I think he knew he was dying and he wanted me to have something from him. For my hope chest, he said." And she made a snorting sound, the closest thing to a laugh that Jim had ever heard from her.

"I can't accept this," Jim said. "You ought to keep this yourself."

"Why?" she said, and her chin came up. "I'm not going to use it for anything. It's not my style."

Jim thought he heard some irony in her voice, but he couldn't see her eyes under the white brim.

"It's not for you," she said. "It's for those children. Did you know that your daughter-in-law's grandmother was my childhood friend?"

"No," Jim said. "I didn't know that."

"Oh, yes," Celie went on. "Elaine Krieger was Elaine Braegger then. That red hair on Roy Krieger runs in the Braegger side of his family, you know. Elaine and I haven't said two words to each other in more than fifty years, not since she married, but we were great friends as girls. She's just my age. I'd like her great-grandchildren to have something from me because it wasn't her fault that we grew apart. It was my fault."

Jim bent forward to look up under the hat brim. Celie began to draw back, but she stopped herself. In her shy smile and clear eyes, Jim could see that she must once have been rather pretty.

"Thank you," he whispered. "It will make very nice curtains." And he put the linen down next to the paint stains on his trousers. "See. I'm painting the inside this sort of light tan, so the cloth will match perfectly."

"Yes, I can see it will," Celie said, already turning toward the gate. About six feet from Jim, she stopped. "I won't be walking out this way so much anymore," she said without looking at him. "I'm going to try some different roads."

"I know what you mean," he said, after a pause. "I've got some new roads I want to try myself. I'll miss you." And it was true.

Celie had almost reached the gate when she turned back toward him.

"The secret is not to be afraid," she called. "You should try not to be afraid."

And she loped across the road, turned right, and headed back for town. Jim watched, holding the package of linen loosely in his hands, until he could see only the crown of her hat, white and blue like some bright flag.

Before the Forgetting

(1991)

Somebody was screaming. Through the walls and closed windows of the room, faintly, she could hear screaming.

"Somebody," she called and was amazed to hear how frail her voice sounded.

"Somebody," she cried a little louder. The plasterboard walls and the single upholstered chair seemed to swallow most of the sound. She waited, looking down at her feet, which didn't quite touch the floor when she was sitting on the bed like this. Waiting was what she always did in this room: waiting for food, waiting for Mary, waiting for sleep.

She was about to call again when the woman who pretended to be Elaine opened the door.

"Did you call me, Ma?" she said, putting just her head into the room.

This business of being called "Ma" was something she'd learned to accept without comment, though she resented it. Over and over, this gaunt old woman would say, "Don't you know me today, Ma? It's Elaine," when, of course, Elaine was a girl, a child.

"I hear somebody screaming."

"That's coming from the fairgrounds. Don't you remember me telling you that this morning? The kids on the rides always scream like that. That's why I closed your windows."

They were always saying, "Don't you remember?" like that, as if she didn't have good sense. She wanted to say, "I remember a lot more than you do, old as you are," but what she actually said was, "I thought it might be Mary."

Now the tall woman came all the way into the room.

"Of course it's not Mary. How could it be Mary?"

"She doesn't come to see me anymore. She hasn't come for a

long time. I think somebody's got her. She might be screaming to get out."

"Try to remember, Mama. Think hard. You know Mary is dead. You went to her funeral last month. It was hot and you wore your blue dress."

She thought, *That's a lie!* But she remembered wearing the blue dress, remembered the church fans swinging back and forth, back and forth on their stands, remembered the flowers moving in the breeze from the fans. The whole church smelled of carnations.

"Mary is dead? My sister is dead?"

"Yes, Ma. Why don't you get up for a while and come out into the living room? It's hot in here with the windows down."

"I don't want to sit in the fan. Drafts are bad for me. People have been killed by drafts, you know."

"Not in the fan, then. You can sit in the armchair and watch a little television."

She let herself be helped up, felt surprise that she seemed unable to move quickly.

Mary was dead. So young, so young. It seemed yesterday that she'd pushed Mary on the board swing, up, up into the apple blossoms. Dead. Grief closed on her, but it had a familiar feel, as if she'd wept already and wouldn't be able to find tears now.

Alone again in the green chair with the television making its meaningless noises, she began to go over in her mind what she knew for sure, a kind of mental game she played after moving from one place to another. Sometimes she even said the list out loud.

"I am Katherine Braegger. My husband is Joe Braegger. My children are Martin, Elaine, Hannah, Angeline, Laura, Ruth, and the twins Robert and Ronald."

People had always raised their eyebrows when she would recite the children's names like that, in the order in which they'd been born. "So many," some would say. "And twins, too."

"We farm a hundred and twenty acres that we got from Pa and we milk forty-two cows and we have water in the house."

In her mind, she could see the house more clearly than the

Winter Roads, Summer Fields

faces of the children, which shifted and changed when she tried to think about one of them. But the ruffled curtains she'd made for the kitchen, the swirl pattern in the linoleum she'd scrubbed so many times on her hands and knees, the stove with its gleaming chrome rail and its enamel knobs on the warming ovens: all of this stood clearly before her squinting eyes.

But what was this place, then? She focused outward onto the room, its rust-colored carpet and flowered sofa. In one corner of the room, there was a card table with a half-finished jigsaw puzzle on it. When Mary came, they played cards on that table, gin rummy, and Mary won most of the time. It was all right, though, because it was so pleasant to sit there in the light from the window, with a glass of ice water winking and dancing in the sun, with Mary's company.

"Sometimes you should let me win just because I'm older than you," she would say.

"Oh, I don't have to let you win," Mary would laugh. "You do that often enough. All those card parties where you took the prizes! You were so good at Schaskopf I was sure the church was going to ban you just like those Vegas casinos I was reading about."

"I don't ever play Schaskopf now. People I used to play with aren't around anymore. And I'm not so good at it now, either."

"Nonsense, Kate! You're the only card player I ever knew who always remembered where all the cards were, in every trick, even in a slow hand."

"Ah. That was before the forgetting. Now I can't remember who took what cards, and it makes me so nervous."

But Mary was dead and Elaine was working on a puzzle. Yes, this was Elaine's house and she lived here now. In the village, in Hammern. The room took on a different meaning as she came to this realization. Photographs on an end table made sense again; there were Elaine's children with their children, pictured with Christmas trees and summer cottages. The needlepoint picture over the sofa was one Elaine had worked on for over a year.

"Elaine," she called, and her voice in her own ears was one she recognized again.

Elaine came from the kitchen carrying a towel. It felt good to see her, as if she'd been away for a long time and had just come home.

"Do you need something, Ma?"

She hadn't thought what she would say; she'd only wanted her in the room. Now she cast around in her mind for something to talk about.

"It's fair time, isn't it?"

"Sure is, Mama," Elaine said and smiled as if she were relieved about something. She came in and sat on the end of the sofa closest to the green chair.

"I'd like to go to the fair again sometime."

Elaine looked down at the towel, but just before her eyes lowered, something like embarrassment had passed over her face.

"It used to be a lot of fun at the fair, but things are different now, Ma. Lots of riffraff. And it's so hot and dusty down there."

Of course, this meant she couldn't go, wouldn't be allowed to go. She felt a flash of resentment, but then reflected that she hadn't really wanted to go to the fair, had only wanted to start a conversation.

"You children used to be a handful when we took you to the buggy races."

"I'll bet we were. Remember the time Ronnie got lost and Papa had to go have him paged over the loudspeaker?"

"You all made yourselves sick eating rich food, and it took a week to get you back to normal."

"That was the rides mostly. You never went on the rides, Mama."

"Oh, I did. When I was a girl, before any of you children came along, your father and I went to the fair. He played in the band then, you know, and he courted me on the Ferris wheel."

"I thought he courted you by taking you home from dances and kermisses."

"Yes, that too. We always had to wait until everybody else was gone because the band had to leave last. Then my pa wanted me in the house as soon as I got home. It was slow courting."

"Well, it worked out in the long run, didn't it?"

"Yes, it did." She looked down at her hands and noted with real sorrow how gnarled and spotted they were; she'd been proud of her hands as a girl—long, slim, white hands that Joe said were perfect, like an angel's hands. And she felt small inside of her clothes now, though she still thought of herself as a tall woman with smooth rounded arms. This loose and folded flesh didn't seem to belong to her.

"I got so old, Elaine. I never thought I would get this old."

"Yes, Mama. Ninety-four is quite an accomplishment."

There was nothing to say to that, for she didn't think of her age as an accomplishment at all. It surprised her that Elaine would say the number out loud like that.

"I have to finish the dishes, Ma. Would you like to come out to the kitchen with me and sit at the table?"

"I could help you."

"No, no, Ma. You can sit and talk to me."

"No. I'll just stay here and watch television. You go along, Elaine."

She might as well watch television as watch someone do dishes. Alone again, she looked not at the flashing display of once-in-a-lifetime bargains, but at the room again, at its emptiness. Sometimes, especially at Christmas, it was filled with people who said they'd come to see her. But they talked to each other or to Elaine, just as if she were not sitting right there in front of them, just as if she'd disappeared. Then she would look at the little ones. She liked some of the quieter children, the ones who looked like her own babies, and she would have liked to make friends with them, but they seemed afraid of her, would hide behind their parents if she motioned for them to come to her lap. There was no way to tell all these people that she didn't want to be here anymore than they did, that she just wanted to go home to the farm, that everything in this place felt like loss.

Of course, there were times, like now, when she knew quite clearly that the farmhouse was gone, torn down and buried in a big hole that Bob had dug just down the hill from the new brick house where he and Linda lived. At these times, she also knew that Joe was gone. She never thought the word "dead" about him, never let it into her mind when she turned her thoughts to Joe. "Gone" was just right because it suggested a destination, a place where she could follow. When she spoke about him to others, she always said, "I lost my husband," because it had the same sound in her mind as "I lost my cookie cutters," the same suggestion that, of course, they were still somewhere in the house, and it was only a matter of time before she found them again.

But the times of knowing things quite clearly were not much comfort to her anymore. There had been a period when the confusion and the forgetting had frightened her badly, made her "nervous," as she would say to Mary. Once she'd looked out the window at a gathering storm and said to Elaine, "You'd better tell Marty to close the barn doors before it starts raining." Almost immediately, she was filled with panic and embarrassment, while Elaine, her face inexplicably old and wrinkled, had looked at her with open mouth and troubled eyes. Then, she'd felt great relief when her mind cleared, just as if clouds had moved aside to let the sunshine in. Mary could always wave the clouds away. "Don't wander, Katie," she would say. "It's so elderly." And then they would laugh softly together at this rich little joke.

But Mary was dead. The carpet under her feet was the wrong color, nothing in the room belonged to her, and there was nothing for her to do—there was absolutely nothing she could do.

So she went looking for the day that was her favorite among all the days. She had to go a long way back to find it, past the years of raising her children, those lightning years that she'd sometimes wished away, only to stand appalled when her wish was granted and the house was emptied of children. Along the way, she paused to glance at some old pains and fears, which had taken on an almost friendly aspect from so many visits. There was Angeline, her face red and puffy from crying. "I don't care what his religion is, Mama. I'm going to marry him and you can't stop me." And Ronnie's leg, when she and Joe had stripped off his overalls, had a piece of bone sticking up through an ugly wound on his thigh. Only when Joe had said, "The doctor doesn't think he'll have a limp," did she move back to the quilting bee where she'd brought all the chattering aunts and neighbors to a silence by saying, "Mama, Joe and I are going to have a baby." That was her first, Martin, little Marty with the carrot-colored hair and the golden-hazel eyes. She could still see the pattern of the quilt and the flowered patch she'd been working on at the time. How grown-up and matronly she'd felt making that announcement in her mother's kitchen! She was twenty years old and already married almost two years.

At last she came to the June day, the sunny afternoon three days after the rain that had interrupted the haying with only one load left to take off the fields. Thin streaks of cloud reached high into the bright blue that arched above the flat, tidy farmlands. The three days had dried the hay and now she and Joe were out with the team and the wagon to bring it in themselves. She stood atop the wagon, dressed in her long cotton skirt and white blouse, her hair bound by a bright yellow scarf that tied at the base of her neck. Joe walked alongside, calling "Giddup" and "Whoa" to the horses as needed. The team, King and Babe, were aging and docile, requiring only voice commands, so the reins were tied loosely to the front of the hayrack. From old habit, the horses walked parallel to the windrows, their big heads bobbing in perfect unison as they pulled.

Every twenty feet, Joe would call to the team to stop. Then he would scoop the dried hay onto a wide fork, carry it to the wagon, and pitch it up. Armed with a smaller fork, she would spread the hay into layers covering all of the wagon bed. Joe hummed and sang snatches of songs and sometimes, when she recognized the tune, she would sing along, but they seldom spoke to each other. It was warm but not uncomfortable, one of those clear, vibrant early summer days.

This particular field was special to both of them, for, in a way, it had been part of her bride-price. When her father had first become aware that she was interested in a horn-playing Irish hired hand, he'd angrily forbidden her to see the boy again.

"What's he doing here?" Pa had asked, scowling. "Who are his people? I don't know any other Irish in these parts. He plays in a band, Katherine! He doesn't own any land. What do you think his prospects are?"

She'd bowed under the storm, but she never gave in. Unless refused permission to go to any wedding dance or coin shower, she was bound to see Joe "by accident" because his band was very popular locally. Finally, the showdown had come, on Easter Sunday afternoon. Dressed in his only suit, his dark hair slicked down and his mustache newly trimmed, his usually laughing eyes serious, Joe presented himself formally to ask permission to court her.

"It's my impression, young man," Pa had said, refusing to answer the question directly, "that Irishmen drink too much, work too little, and don't make very faithful husbands."

From her vantage point on the large horsehair sofa, she could tell by the set of his face that her father didn't mean this as a cruelty, but as a test, to see if Joe had a temper. Joe smiled, a truly good-natured smile, before he answered.

"Your impression may not be altogether wrong, for I've known some men to be like that. Not all of them Irish either. But that isn't any part of me. You can ask George Kelnofer about me. He's had no cause for complaint in the two years I've worked for him. As to the drinking, I take a beer now and then, but I don't overdo it, and I never take hard liquor at all. And I will make Kate a faithful, loving husband, for I love her dearly."

Though a little embarrassed by the last part of this speech, Pa was favorably impressed, she could tell.

"I'll make you a bargain, fella," he said. "There's a ten-acre field at the far side of my property that's never been cleared. It's not a woods, but it has quite a few trees on it. If you can clear that field, use the wood to build a house, and get some small grain harvest off of it by next summer, you will prove my impression wrong."

"And then I can marry Kate?" Joe asked cheerfully, completely unimpressed by the enormous task that had been handed him.

"Well, I suppose so, yes." Pa had been caught off guard by the quick response.

All that summer and fall, she'd slipped over to watch Joe, who took a few hours off whenever the Kelnofers could spare him to chop away at the trees, using a borrowed team to drag the logs to the little knoll above the creek. In the evenings, after doing the milking at the Kelnofers's, he would come back with some of his friends from the band to work on the house until full dark. All of them sang loud, funny songs while they worked, and she and Mary would help where they could, furnishing food and drink smuggled out of the bulging pantry next to their mother's kitchen.

The tree stumps posed the biggest problem, threatening to take a lot of time to dig and pull out. Pa said he didn't think Joe would ever get it done before the snow began to fly. When she told him this, Joe hummed a little and smiled. Finally, one day in early October, he stopped at the big house to ask if she and Mary could come out to watch him remove the stumps. Pa had looked him over from head to toe as if he thought he must have gone silly, but he let them go along.

Joe made them sit on the hilltop behind his roughly framed house, and then he strode off, carrying a large canvas sack. They could see him squat down beside a stump, reach into the bag, and place something into a hole as deep as the length of his arm. After a moment or two of some activity they couldn't see, he sprang up, snatched the sack, and ran toward them. About thirty feet from them, he flopped down behind a stump just as a tremendous sound erupted from the ground and a shower of dirt and wood chips burst upward into the cool afternoon sky. Joe stood up, grinning and holding the sack aloft. "Dynamite," he shouted.

Back and forth he went, walking up to a stump, running away, flopping and rolling like a playful child, always turning back toward them after each blast as if expecting applause. After about a half hour, drawn by the noise, Pa joined them on the hill to watch, his face expressionless, but his eyes twinkling.

By mid-winter, Pa had found the time to help Joe work on the inside of the house, offering advice about the well, and going all the way into Green Bay with Joe to bring back a pump. In the spring, Joe seeded the field. He put in oats and clover seed at the same time, knowing the grain harvest the first year would give way to rich hay by the second year.

The wedding was in August and Joe's band played for the dance. Once, around midnight, Joe sat down to play a number with them, his last performance.

So now, married just over ten months, they were taking in the first hay crop from Joe's field. They'd almost reached the little oasis in the center of the field, the one green spot in ten acres of browned stubble and dried hay. Joe had left one tree, a gigantic oak whose spreading boughs created almost a quarter acre of shade.

"I know it's impractical, in the middle of the field and all," he'd sighed, "but I just can't bring myself to go chopping at it. It's such a lovely thing and older than all of us put together. We'll just let it have its little spot."

The horses were looking pensively at the shade and the bright wild grasses under the tree, but they were too well behaved to make any move toward it on their own. Joe lifted a forkful of hay to Kate's feet. She hadn't even raised her own fork when she saw the bundle move and then quicken into life. An unmistakable brown and golden shape detached itself from the background of identically colored hay.

In swift reflex, she scooped the snake onto the fork and threw

Winter Roads, Summer Fields

it away from her, into a shower of falling hay. Through it, she could see Joe's face lifting toward her, just beginning to look surprised, and then both hay and snake landed on his shoulders. The snake flexed once, glinting in the sun, and then disappeared inside Joe's overall bib.

"Hey!" he cried. The horses made one little jerk and then settled down again. Joe began to slap at his clothes, jumping and twisting, but making no more sounds. In a kind of fascinated horror, frozen, she watched his silent dance, until a flicker at his shoes caught her attention. The snake, a harmless king snake, streaked off into the windrow. But Joe hadn't seen it go, hadn't felt it go. He was still jumping, had begun to open his overall bib.

"It's gone, Joe," she called to him.

"I can feel it," he answered, pulling the overalls down over his lean hips, looking inside the pants legs and stamping his feet.

"I saw it go into the windrow," she said, beginning to giggle.

He'd stripped the overalls off his shoes before this registered with him.

"You saw it?" he asked, looking up at her.

"Yes, over there," she pointed, sobering her face. "It was only a king snake. And a little one too."

He stood there with the overalls in his left hand, his white legs making a sharp contrast to his sun-darkened arms and face, and he blushed, a deep red spreading under the tan around his eyes.

"Katie Braegger," he said. "Did you do that on purpose?"

"Of course not! Did you throw it up here on purpose?"

"Certainly not. I never knew it was there."

For a second or two, they looked at each other, and then both of them began to laugh, a great outburst of laughter that made the horses turn their heads back over their shoulders. Joe finally got breath enough to speak.

"Goodness! I thought for a minute there that I was going to have to call St. Patrick back down out of his blessed home in heaven to do for me what he did for Ireland."

Before the Forgetting

"Don't be irreverent. A man without his pants shouldn't be calling on any saints."

"Come down here, my Katie. As long as I'm already half undressed, we might as well take a little rest."

She slid down and he led the horses over the windrow to the shade of the oak. She pulled off the scarf, letting her hair tumble free.

"Well, Kate. You may as well get out of that long, hot skirt."

"Joe Braegger!"

"Come along, girl. We're in the middle of our own field, under our very own tree, and there's no one around for more than a mile. Who's to see you?"

She moved closer to the tree, feeling the cool grasses against her ankles. She looked out over the field in all directions.

"Well, I suppose," she said, loosening the ties at her waist. The skirt fell around her feet and she stepped out of it.

"It would be cooler without the blouse too," he said, stepping up to her with a little smile playing around his mouth.

"You've still got your shirt on."

Without a word and without looking away from her eyes, he unbuttoned his shirt and pulled it off. Then, gently, he began to unbutton her blouse from the top while she unbuttoned it from the bottom. When she stood only in her shift, he took her hands and sat down, pulling her onto the grass next to him.

"Joe. Do you think we should? Outside?"

"Why certainly, my beauty. It's earth's own sweet bed, isn't it?"

He ran his fingers down the inside of her arm from elbow to wrist and brushed his mustache against her bare shoulder in the way that always made her shiver. Then he stretched back full length into the grass.

"My beautiful Katie," he murmured, and his voice was like a song. "Come down here to me."

She bent slowly down to his chest, her cheek and mouth coming to rest in the coarse hair. From somewhere in the field there came the high, lilting song of a meadowlark, rising and falling, while the horses chomped away at the wildflowers at the edge of the oasis. The harness buckles jingled like bells.

Huddled down inside the green arm chair, she'd found her way back to that moment, could see and hear it all again. She had left behind the strange room in a stranger's house to live in the time before everything got lost. And it was sweet, so sweet that she never wanted to leave it again. Never.

Families of
Hammern Township

LANZER FAMILY TREE

Herman Lanzer (1881–1939) + Ida Merens (1885–1963)

Nicholas (1916–) + Loretta Duescher, lost contact with family in 1946
whereabouts of children unknown

Cecilia (1920–)

Farm sold in 1963; present site of Davister's raceway.

TOMCHEK FAMILY TREE

Isador Tomchek (1888–1968) + Mary Schwab (1893–1975)

Wencil (Jim) (1914–) + Emma Lensmeier (1920–)
5 children, all now living in Oregon

George (1916–) + Laura Kollross (1917–)
John (1941–1960) killed in car accident
Sharon (1952–) + Andrew Paulson (1950–) marriage dissolved in 1980
Lisa (1974–)

Tomchek farm sold in 1982 to Roman Grassel, who farms it now.

BRAEGGER FAMILY TREE

Joseph Braegger (1984–1969) + Katherine Schroeder (1897–)

Martin (1918–) + Evelyn Weinfurter (1921–)
    4 children

Elaine (1920–) + Peter Krieger (1918–)
    Roy (1939–) + Marian Pauly (1938–)
        Jeffrey (1961–1968) died of leukemia
        Lee Ann (1964–) + William Mueller (1963–)
            Michael (1986–)
            Joanna (1988–)
            Molly (1989–)
        Julie (1968–) + Harold Arenz
        David (1973–)
        John (1976–)
    Elizabeth (1940–) + Thomas Sensbauer (1938–)
    Katherine (1946–) + Carl Kelnofor (1945–)
    Joseph (1948–)

Hannah (1921–) + Robert Duchateau (1919–)
    6 children

Angeline (1923–) + Albert Olson (1921–)
    2 children

Laura (1926–) became Sister Mary Bernadette in 1948,
                left the order in 1965

Ruth (1930–) + Thomas Rentmeester (1931–)
    5 children

Robert (twin) (1932–) + Linda Daul (1938–) still farming Braegger land
    3 children

Ronald (twin) (1932–) + Harriet Estel (1933–)
    4 children

MUELLER FAMILY TREE

Matthew Mueller (1912–1971) + Rose Schroeder (1914–1986)
(second cousin to Katherine Schroeder
Braegger)

James (1935–) + Joanna Bower (1936–)
Barbara (1961–) + David Hemmings (1958–)
now living in California with 2 children
William (1963–) + Lee Ann Krieger (1964–)
Michael (1986–)
Joanna (1988–)
Molly (1989–)

Mueller farm now run by William Mueller.

SENSBAUER FAMILY TREE

Luke Sensbauer (1913–) + Ruth Flegel (1914–1980)

Thomas (1938–) + Elizabeth (Betsy) Krieger (1940–)
David (1963–)
Donald (1965–)
Dennis (1967–)

Mark (1940–) + Sandra Bartel (1942–)
now living in Arizona with 4 children

Benjamin (1944–1968) killed in Vietnam

Sensbauer farm now run by Thomas and Dennis.

HIMRICH FAMILY TREE

Jacob Himrich (1919-) + Anna Baye (1918-)

Henry (1947-) + Louise Colle (1948-)
John (1975-)
Eric (1977-)

Frances (1950-)

James (1951-1958) died of complications of measles

Paul (1954-) + Cynthia Kollross (1958-)
(niece of Laura Kollross Tomchek)
Jennifer (1983-)
Paul, Jr. (1986-)

Farm sold in October of 1983; present site of Eastbrook golf course.

FREDERICK FAMILY TREE

George Frederick (1926-) + Helen Christoff (1929-1977)

Robert (1948-) + Carol Braegger (1947-)
(daughter of Martin Braegger)
Sarah (1973-)
Jason (1974-)

Margart (1951-) + Anthony Johnson (1951-)
Alyssa (adopted 1982)
Mya (adopted 1985)

Elaine (1957-) + Frank Pankratz (1958-)
Amy (1978-)
Alex (1982-)

Todd (1963-) + Mary Koenig (1963-) currently farming the Frederick land
Helen (1990-)

Marjorie Dorner is the author of another book of literary fiction, *Seasons of Sun and Rain* (Milkweed Editions, 1999), and several mysteries, including *Blood Kin* (Morrow, 1992), *Freeze Frame* (Morrow, 1990), *Family Closets* (McGraw-Hill, 1989) and *Nightmare* (McGraw-Hill, 1987). She earned her Ph.D. in English Literature from Purdue University and currently lives in Minnesota.

Interior design by R. W. Scholes
Typeset in Caslon 76
by Stanton Publication Services
Printed on acid-free 55# Glatfelter Natural paper
by Bang Printing